Just Me.

Morley.

Jacquelyn Johnson

Cataloguing in Publication Data

Jacquelyn Johnson

Just Me. Morley.

Description: Crimson Hill Books trade paperback edition | Nova Scotia, Canada

ISBN:	978-1-989595-35-0 (Paperback - Ingram)
BISAC:	YAF000000 Young Adult Fiction: General YAF022000 Young Adult Fiction: Girls & Women YAF058020 Young Adult Fiction: Social Themes – Bullying
THEMA:	FXB – Narrative Theme: Coming of age YXO -- Children's / Teenage personal & social issues: Bullying, violence, abuse & peer pressure YXHB -- Children's / Teenage personal & social issues: Friends & friendship issues

Record available at https://www.bac-lac.gc.ca/eng/Pages/home.aspx

Front Cover Image: Cristina Zabolotnii

Book Design & Formatting: Jesse Johnson

Parts of this story formerly appeared in the novel Morley & Feather published in 2019.

Crimson Hill Books
(a division of)
Crimson Hill Products Inc.
Wolfville, Nova Scotia
Canada

Crimson Hill
Books

All Morley Star wants is to be allowed to adopt the kitten she rescued and for her stepfather to come home.

When it looks like neither wish will be granted, she mounts a plan to get her family back to the happy place they used to be.

Can making armloads of wish bracelets, baking carloads of cookies, standing up to mean girl Julia and volunteering at the pet shelter possibly help?

Or is it going to take something even more powerful than all this for Morley to make her wishes come true?

A heartwarming story about being a modern girl who dreams big, the true meaning of friendship and families and how they change, first in a new series for readers ages 10 to 13.

Also In
The Morley Stories
Series:

Just Me. Morley

Feather's Girl

Sam's Gift

Rules for Flying

Find them all at
www.CrimsonHillBooks.com

Somewhere over the rainbow

Skies are blue

And the dreams that you dare to
dream

Really do come true.

Someday I'll wish upon a star

And wake up where the clouds are far

Behind me

Where troubles melt like lemon drops

Away above the chimney tops

That's where you'll find me.

*-"Somewhere Over The Rainbow"
by Harold Arlen and Yip Harburg,
as sung by Judy Garland.*

one

It's a Happy Friday. In April.

"C'mon, kiddo," mom says, not turning away from the stove. She's stirring something for supper that's making my mouth water.

In our family, all the days have names. Fridays are happy because it's the start of the weekend.

Mondays are Morley Mondays. That's the day I make our supper. Something easy to do, like mac and cheese. Or grilled cheese sandwiches and soup. Or beans on toast.

Tuesdays are Daisy Days. That means my sister gets to pick what we have.

Wednesdays are Veggie Wednesdays. That's the day we generally have salad, because it's easy.

Thursdays are for eating out. Mom usually takes us to

The Salty Dog because kids under 12 eat free on Thursdays.

Weekends are the best. Saturdays are my day to say what we'll have. I almost always ask mom to make home-made waffles, with maple syrup. And bacon.

Sundays mom gets to choose what we have. She usually makes a lot of it, so we can have it for our bag lunches all week.

But today is a Friday, so she's cooking something that smells like curry.

It seems like five minutes since I started drawing. But now she's going, "OK, Morley. Time to pack up and get a move on!"

The drawing I'm working on is a picture of my friend Jayden riding Spirit. Spirit is his horse. It has to be especially good, because this picture is for his 11th birthday. And that's tomorrow.

Mom gave me a frame for it. It's one of her yard sale finds. I've already sanded it and painted it. We bought a new piece of glass and a picture mat to fit. So, it's ready to put together and wrap, as soon as this drawing is finished.

Mom said she'd help frame it when it's done.

But something still isn't right about this drawing. Is it the way Spirit is raising his head? Or is it Jayden's face? Or is it the background?

I can't decide what's wrong. It looks like Jayden and Spirit, but it doesn't. It's really bugging me that I don't know why. It isn't much use asking my mom, because all she says is, "Oh, I'm sure Jayden will love it because it's from you and you're such good friends."

That's no help at all.

I totally hate quitting in the middle of doing something, especially when it's a drawing or painting and I'm trying to get it to be *brilliant*.

But it's not working.

And it needs to be done.

"And where's your sister?" mom calls out as I'm heading down the hall to what used to be the playroom. "Tell her supper's ready!"

I sigh, realizing I have no idea where Crazy Daisy is right now. But, as mom always says, I'm almost eleven and the oldest. That means my little sister is My Responsibility.

I hope Daisy's in the room we share, but that isn't likely. For one thing, I can't hear her making noise anywhere. For another, she hasn't interrupted me, like, a million times to get her a snack or make the remote work or let her use my markers or *who knows what else.*

I live with my mother and little sister in a small town where not much ever happens. I do all the regular kid things, for somebody in grade 5. I'm not the most popular kid, or the one who always gets the best grades, or the one who's good at sports, or anything special.

My best friend Jayden is special at riding horses. It's like he knows how to talk to them without even saying one word!

My other best friend, Sam, who's a girl, is special at playing the piano and the violin. Or pretty much any musical instrument she gets interested in. She's got a bunch of awards for how good her playing is. Her parents really want her to be a concert pianist when she's older. Or maybe that's just her mom. She doesn't see her dad very often, because he lives in California.

Jayden lives on a farm. He loves animals, like his mother, who's a vet, which is another name for a doctor for animals. He's got five older brothers and so many cousins, I don't know all their names. Some of them work with his dad and uncles on their farm. So that's probably what he'll do, too.

I don't have a clue what I'll do when I grow up.

My Mum says she doesn't care what Daisy and I do, just so long as we grow up to be good people who are happy. And doing what she calls "contributing to society." Whatever that is.

Sometimes, I feel like I'm almost invisible.

Being invisible has advantages. For one thing, you can learn things just by watching people. They do and say things that maybe they don't mean to.

Maybe it's because I like to draw that I also like to look really closely at things. Especially people. I want to get it exactly right when I draw them or paint them.

Or write about them.

There are four people in our family. Or three, right now. Me. Mom. Daisy. The fourth one is Danny, who's my stepfather, but he's not with us right now. He's gone to the city to find work.

Daisy is never invisible. She's the kind of little kid who's always doing some airy-fairy thing. You can pretty much always tell where she is because she's REALLY UNBELIEVABLY LOUD. ALL the time.

I listen to see if she's pounding on the piano in the living room. Or yelling on her swing out front. Or screaming on the trampoline out back. Or just roaring around in the yard. Or watching TV in the living room. She always turns it up loud.

I can't hear any kind of Daisy noise right now. But then, I usually try to tune her out. Ever since getting home, I've been drawing in my sketchbook and not saying much to mom, who's been baking cookies and banana bread and a pie and then stirring something on the stove for dinner.

It's not a good sign. The baking, I mean.

Baking is what our mother does when she's upset about something. She bakes. A lot. Lately, that's so much that we can't possibly eat it all even though it's all delicious. I think she mostly shoves all her baking in the freezer. Or gives it away to the church bake sale or the women's crisis shelter or other people where she works.

They're all probably pretty happy about all this baking, but I'm not. When she's baking, she's not the mostly happy mother we're used to.

The room I have to share now with Daisy is what used to be called the crafts and playroom. That was before the renters got the whole entire upstairs of our house.

They got all the bedrooms, the bathroom with the big corner tub, our family room, the alcove with my drawing desk and the little balcony at the front.

After Danny lost his job and got arrested by the police and couldn't find another job, mom and Danny shoved my bed and Daisy's and both our dressers into the crafts and playroom. So now that's our bedroom. They turned the dining room into their bedroom. Now the dining room table is crowded into one end of the living room and our family is crammed into the bottom half of our house.

Those renters are a menace!

They clomp up and down the stairs all day long. Their baby cries all the time, especially at night. Worst of all, the man renter shouts and swears a lot. The lady renter shouts back and screams and cries a lot.

Mom says take no notice, that's just the way they are, but sometimes I have a hard time making myself not hear them.

I also try not to care too much about the mess in the room I share with Daisy. Mom says it's ridiculous, to get upset about such a little thing as a few toys lying around. She says any sensible person knows there's far more important things to worry about.

To me, mess IS an important thing. The floor is covered with Daisy's toys, game pieces, dolls, sticker books, fairy dresses, shoes, socks, underwear, pajamas, boots and JUNK.

It feels like there isn't enough air to breathe in our room because all the space is taken up with her stuff. I'm always picking up in there. I like things to be neat and where I can find them. It really upsets me when my things get lost. Or Daisy breaks them.

But no matter what I do, our room is always the same crazy Daisy mess. I try not to step on her stuff while clearing a path over to my bed so I can put my art supplies away on a high shelf where Daisy won't get into them. I hope.

I really miss having my own space, just exactly the way I want it, where I can draw, or read, or just look up at the little shiny stars mom painted on the ceiling of my old room. It used to be so quiet there, at the top of our house where the ceiling is slant-y, the walls are painted my favourite night-sky blue and my desk just fits in front of the window.

Out that window, I could see a part of our garden and, way out in the distance, just a tiny silvery sliver of the Atlantic Ocean. At night, with the window open, I can just about imagine hearing the waves rolling in and the gulls calling to each other.

At my desk in front of that window was always my favorite place to be.

But now the renters have my room. And Daisy's. And mom's, too. And the upstairs living room. And the balcony.

Here's my plan. We need to get Danny back so Mum can be happy again. Those renters will have to go live someplace else. I don't care where. Then there'll be no more having to listen to them yelling and fighting all the time.

I'll get my own room back. We'll get our home back, for our family.

And maybe mom won't be upset all the time, so she'll do less baking.

That's my big wish, one of them. That our family can be like it was before all the bad luck happened.

When our mom didn't worry that her job isn't enough. That's what she said. The not-enough part isn't about the work she does, she said. There's more than enough of that. It's about not-enough-money.

Here's how mom explained it.

Grown-ups do jobs to earn money to pay for everything we have, like a nice place to live, food to eat, the clothes we wear and a car or a bus pass to get around and do errands. Or go to the beach.

Once you've lost your job, mom said, you can't just find it again. It's not like misplacing your door key or your bathing suit or looking everywhere for your favourite winter scarf before it finally turns up in the last place you look.

Which makes sense, when you think about it. Something that's lost is always in the last place you look, because when you find a thing, that's when you stop looking for it.

When a job is lost, it doesn't ever get found again. It just stays lost. You have to go find another job. A different job, near where you live if you're lucky. Or maybe further away.

Like Danny going to the city to find a new job. I don't understand how him getting a new job in the city means he can come home and live with us, but when I ask mom, she says she doesn't want to talk about it right now.

She says it's best to think about something else. Something more pleasant.

I want our family to go back to when we lived in our whole house and Danny knew exactly where his job was, which was selling cars. The time when we were a family together. When my mom didn't look so worried and sad.

Sometimes, it feels like what we do most of is wait.

Wait for the renters to quieten down, so we can sleep.

Wait for Danny to call or send an email, so we know he's OK and when he's coming home.

Wait for some good luck to happen.

So, here's my first BIG wish. Danny comes home. Life gets OK again. We're happy. Like we used to be.

My second BIG wish is to get a pet. A real pet. One you can play with, like a dog. Or a cat. Not like a fish, because all they do is swim around their bowl. Then they die.

And not like the lizard that's our classroom pet in Mrs. Green's class, because lizards are interesting to watch, but you can't actually play with them very much.

A cat is the pet I really want, but a dog would be fun, too, I think. Maybe like Sparky, the dog we had when I was a baby, so I don't really remember him at all.

But I know we had him, because there are pictures of me when I was little playing with Sparky. He was a medium-sized dog with rough white fur with some brown patches. He looked like he was smiling all the time.

Which is why I don't get it when mom says, "No pets, Morley!" every time I try to talk to her about it. Even though I've seen photos of Sparky.

Him sitting next to me in my highchair.

Us playing on the floor.

Our family did have a pet, once. Why can't we have one now?

Mom has a lot of answers, like we don't have enough space for a pet and pets get fleas and pets shed hair and they cost money and you need to be more responsible before you get a pet.

I try to tell her that I am responsible.

I'd take good care of our pet.

I'd feed them and clean up if they make a mess.

They wouldn't get fleas because they'd get flea medicine. If they were sick, we'd take them to Jayden's mum. Dr. Van Haan.

Pets take up hardly any space, especially one little cat, but mom just keeps saying we have a NO Pets Rule in our house. Even through the renters have a kitten.

I know, because I hear it sometimes.

No, mom says, that's just their baby. I don't think that's true, because I know there's a kitten upstairs.

I've heard that baby crying.

I've also heard the kitten, in my head. It's not like little kitten meows. It's more like colors, or pictures of feelings. It's not words like "warm," or "hungry," or "sleepy."

Maybe he's still too young to know any words.

I know it's the kitten, but when I try to tell mom this, all she says is "Don't be silly, Morley! Cats don't talk in your head. So just stop it and act your age!"

So, I have. Stopped telling her, I mean, not stopped hearing the kitten. It's like gentle whispering, not in my ear but right inside my head.

I can't hear him when I'm at school. Or any time except when I'm at home, so maybe I have to be close to him to hear him. I know it's a he, this kitten, but I don't know his name. And here's the truth; I've never even seen him.

But I know he's sweet and I wish he was ours.

I think having a pet is just part of being a real family. Me, Daisy, Mom, Danny and our family cat. Or dog. Or maybe even two pets. A dog AND a cat.

I don't care what colour coat they have, or what type of dog or cat they are, or even if they're a boy or a girl. I might even let Daisy name him. Or her. If we could have a pet.

Mom is right about one thing. The way our messy room looks right now, there isn't room for even one little cat bed. It's full of too much stuff all over the place. Right at this moment our messy room is also quiet, meaning no Daisy.

She must be outside. Winter is almost over, but it's still wet out. And cold. But at least all the snow is gone, all melted away leaving the ground brown and squishy. The trees are waiting to get dressed up in their new leaves.

I grab my coat off the hook by the back door. I'm careful not to let it slam.

Daisy is nowhere in sight. And it's starting to get dark.

Our backyard is not much wider than our house, but it slopes down and goes way back. From the front of our house, you'd never know there's so much yard back there. It is absolutely the coolest thing about living at our house.

In summer there are flowers and a vegetable garden near the house and then some trees and a patch of grass and then a row of lilacs.

Beyond that, there's the trampoline, then a lot of space we don't really use that used to be a lawn, but now it's more like a wild meadow with a path through it and little secret places with benches to sit. Mom wanted to have a goat and maybe some chickens, but we live in town, so they don't let you.

Which I think is just another stupid rule!

At the very back there are trees and then a little trickle of a stream, too small for swimming in or fishing or anything useful. But it looks pretty. There are frogs and minnows in it. And sometimes Daisy, in her princess rain boots, but she's not there right now.

Next to the stream is my favourite thing about our yard. It's a huge apple tree, all rough and gnarly because it's ancient. It might be 200 years old, or even older, Danny says. This old tree has a falling-down treehouse that somebody built before we lived here. The treehouse is as high up as the balcony on the front of our house.

From up in the treehouse, you can see all our back yard and garden, all the way up the hill to the house.

Last summer, my mother helped me fix up the treehouse. I put some old cushions in it and some of my books and a couple of my drawings are pined to the walls. There's a tin with cookies in it, and some juice boxes. In summer, sometimes I go up there to hang out with Sam and Jayden. It's a good place to get away from Daisy.

Danny is pretty hopeless about fixing anything. But our mother is the opposite. She believes in fixing things or what she calls re-purposing them. This means you don't throw things out. You fix them and use them. Or sell them. Or give them to someone who needs them. She says there's always a use for a thing. And that waste is a sin.

She's always painting a piece of furniture she found in a yard sale, or making a dusty old lamp work again, or sewing cushion covers or curtains for the living room. Or painting the walls "just to brighten things up."

Mom is the one who taught me how to climb a ladder,

how to hammer in nails and how to sand and paint things so they look new again.

She's also the one who showed me how to knit and crochet and string beads. Like me, she loves all that artsy-craftsy stuff.

Another cool thing about our mother is her job is being the school secretary, so she gets holidays and all summer off like Daze and me. That's when we have time to do crafts together (which I love) or gardening (which is just OK) or go to the beach (Daisy's favourite). It's when my birthday is and totally the best time of year.

And, this summer, also when mom says Danny might be coming back. *Might*, she says. That would be exactly one half of my secret wishes magically coming true!

Thinking this makes me smile.

Even right now, when I'm trudging all the way to the back of our yard, calling Daisy's name, telling her come on, supper's ready. And getting soakers, because I forgot to put on my boots.

Daisy doesn't answer.

And now it's really starting to rain. I reach into my pockets. I find old used tissues. A folded piece of paper. A quarter. Pocket fuzz. That's all. My gloves aren't there.

I'm getting wet. And cold. And hungry.

"Daisy," I keep yelling. I'm all the way at the very back of our property now, where I know it isn't possible to see from where mom's probably watching from the kitchen window. "Come on, where are you?"

Then she giggles, and I look up.

And there she is, up in the apple tree, sitting on the very edge of the little deck of the tree-house. "Fooled you, Morley!" she calls down to me. "Bet you didn't know I can get up here, but I can. Just like you!"

"Come on down!" I yell, but all she says is, "Can't!"

I look around for the rope ladder, but there's no sign of it.

"Come on," I holler. "Get the ladder and climb down! Mom says we have to come for supper right NOW!"

Daisy just laughs and stands up, right at the edge, holding the rope ladder. It's broken, so now it's just one rope, with some sticks hanging off it. I don't know how that could've happened, but I don't stop to figure it out.

I have no idea how she got up there. Right now, Daisy needs to get down.

But how? There aren't any low branches on the apple tree, so there's no way to climb up to the treehouse without the ladder.

Or *a* ladder.

Then I remember that there's a ladder in the garage. It's made out of metal so it's too long and heavy for me to carry all this way, but I can balance it on the wheelbarrow and push it back here. Or get mom to help.

"Sit down RIGHT NOW!" I shout up to Daisy. "STAY THERE. I'll get the ladder from the garage and get you down. But you have to WAIT till I go get it."

"Don't want to!" she says, in her sing-song-y voice. "Silly old Morley. You're not the boss of me!" and she's standing up now, dancing around and trying to do a handstand on the little deck above me.

Even though it's raining and that treehouse deck must be slippery.

She's really starting to frighten me. Daisy is always what Danny calls, "a real little dare-devil." She isn't afraid of heights, or the dark, or monsters under the bed, or witches hiding in her closet, or getting a bad report card.

Or anything.

Daisy usually has band-aids on her knees, but she doesn't seem to care. With all her dare-devil stunts like trying to hold her breath underwater for longer than me, or ride her bicycle no hands, or do skateboard tricks, or when she jumped off the top bunk, so mom made Danny take the bunk beds apart, she never gets hurt.

Not really.

Mom is always telling Daisy to just behave, missy, or she'll be sorry.

Danny always just laughs and says Daisy is like him, easy-going and up for anything. She's got his Irish luck, he says.

What he also says, that Daisy's more like him and I'm

more like mom, might be true.

"Look at me, Morley!" Daisy shouts now. "I'm a famous acrobat! Catch me, Morley. I'll do a trick and you have to catch me, just like Daddy does!"

That's her thing, being an acrobat. It started after she saw some acrobats on *America's Got Talent*. Before that, she wanted to be a ski jumper in the Olympics, or an ice dancer and do all those spins and jumps and leaps and throws through the air.

Or a race car driver, or an astronaut. Mom says she'll grow out of all that foolishness eventually.

Danny thinks it's hilarious.

He'd get her down. Or catch her.

But he isn't here.

I am.

And I know this is crazy dangerous.

"No, Daisy. Don't. Please. Just wait. PLEASE. Sit down and stay still! I'll get you down, as soon as I go get the ladder! Just STAY there!"

"NO-ooooooooooooooh" Daisy shrieks.

As I turn to go back to the house, fetch the ladder, tell mom, then hurry back here, working out in my head how fast I can possibly do all these things, I look back and Daisy isn't on the deck anymore.

She's flying through the air, arms and legs spread out, like a snow angel pasted on the sky. And she's laughing like crazy.

It's as if she's flying.

Without even thinking, I try to catch her.

two

Maybe I remember what happened next, but it's all mixed up in my head. I kind of know, but it could all be what someone told me. When I woke up.

Or it could have been a dream I had. A bad one.

Or even something I sort of remember seeing on TV or in a movie. Or reading in a book.

I just don't know for sure.

There's this sort of picture in my head of the ground being close to me. It's really hard and rough, like a rock. And so cold.

I'm on that rock. I'm trying to get up, but I can't. It's like my legs don't work. And there is someone screaming, but I don't know who. Not words, just screaming.

Maybe it's a siren. Or some animal howling. Or just

the wind. I wish it would stop. It's hurting my head.

Then there are a lot of voices. All talking at the same time. Really far away. I can't hear what they're saying.

The first thing I do know for sure is I'm lying on something hard, but smooth.

Cool-ish.

Not cold.

A bed, it must be.

But not my bed.

So, are we on vacation? But we never go on vacation. Mom says it's because we already live near the ocean where people come for vacations, thousands of them every year. And we're so lucky to live here. Why would we ever want to go someplace else?

Our family isn't on vacation. We're not visiting relatives like grandad or somewhere that isn't home.

So, why am I lying on this strange hard bed at...

At where?

I need to get up.

I really need to pee.

But everything hurts.

I can't make myself sit up.

My head is pounding.

I feel dizzy and like I'm going to throw up.

What's totally strange is that my eyes don't want to open.

But why? I try to work it out, but my head feels like someone is playing the drums in there.

Thinking is just too hard to do right now.

It hurts to even just lie still and breath. All I can do is take quick, tiny little sips of air.

I try moving my legs. They seem to be OK. So is my left arm, but not my right. I can't move my right hand. When I try to move my arm, even a little bit, a pain shoots through it up to my shoulder.

This is scary.

It feels like the crashing and banging headache behind my eyes has spread to everywhere in my body.

I try to talk. But this little moan-y sound, like a sick dog that's whining, is all that comes out.

Some time goes by. I don't know how long, but I must have gone to sleep.

Then, oddly, it's day-time. My eyes are open. I'm looking around at the strangest room I've ever been it.

It's tiny. Only just big enough for this odd bed, a plain chair like you see in waiting rooms at the dentist and a window that looks out at a parking lot, where it's raining. The sky is gray.

Everything in that room except me is white. Everything. White walls, white ceiling, white sheets, white blanket. This room needs some drawings or paintings on the walls. It needs something that's in colour. And alive.

"Ah, I see you're back with us," someone says. A woman, I notice now, in a pale blue nurse dress. Suddenly, she's there, right next to my bed.

But what is she doing here, in this odd room?

Who is she?

I wonder if she'll tell me.

"Can you tell me your name, dear?" she says. I think about how I'd draw her. In a garden. Not in this white room.

"Your name? she says, leaning closer, touching my left hand. "Do you know it?"

Doesn't everyone know their own name unless they're a baby? But I try to answer.

But I try to answer

"Mor. Ley. Jane. Eliz. Abeth," I say. It comes out in puffs, sounding like a croaky-whisper.

"Good. And your last name?"

"It's...Star..." There's a stabbing feeling in my chest as I try to get enough air to talk. "Morley. Star."

"Very good. And where do you live, Morley Jane Elizabeth Star?"

"Seabright."

"And how old are you, Morley?"

It hurts to talk. "Why ... you asking... questions? And ...

who... are you?" I say. This conversation is making me so tired, I wish I was still asleep.

Then I have this idea. I could pretend to be asleep. But I still need to know things.

Important things, like where am I?

Why aren't I at home? Or at school?

Why does my whole body hurt and my head feel like it's pounding and stuffed with wet paper?

Why is everything so strange?

Why does it hurt so bad when I breathe?

Shouldn't I be checking to see if Daisy is still mooning around or if she's just about dressed for school?

And getting myself ready?

Why am I here, all alone in this strange place, talking to a stranger?

But then everything seems to be getting foggy and far away.

I can hear the nurse-woman say words like "an accident" and "caring for you" and "hospital" and "your mother." There might be something about "buzzer," but I don't know what she means. Why would there be a buzzer? Is this a game show? Her voice is getting softer and softer, more like whispering.

Like we're underwater.

Then I can't hear anything at all but a shushing sound. Like the sounds the ocean makes at the shore. Big waves roar in. They break on the shore. Then they melt back into the ocean.

I think what a lovely sound it is.

We're at the beach. It's a hot day.

Danny and Mum are spread out on their beach chairs, talking about something and she's laughing. Me and Daisy are running in and out of the water and we're laughing too.

Then we're looking for sea-glass where the sand is still wet as the tide goes out. That's the best place to find it. Right at the water edge. Especially right after a storm.

Sea glass is just broken bits of bottles that end up in the sea. The sea tosses these broken pieces around and grinds them into rounded shapes.

Lots of people collect sea glass to put in a jar, for a decoration. Or to make into jewellery. Or, what Daisy likes to do, paste pieces on paper to make pictures.

There just was a storm. I just remembered. It was raining. Hard.

I was outside. It was raining.

Almost dark.

And cold.

But where was that? Why was I there? Where was everyone else? Were we at the beach with mom and Danny?

But why, in a storm?

Storms bring sea glass. And that's what we find, my sister and I. Beautiful pieces that are blues and greens and clear and milky white and my very most favourite, amber glass, which is dark orange. One of the rarest colours of sea glass you can find. It means good luck, when you do find amber sea glass. Like finding a four-leaf clover. Or seeing a shooting star. Or a rainbow.

Daisy helps me search for a while, but then, there are some people at the beach with a happy dog and she wants to run and play with the dog.

But now mom is calling for Daisy and she's calling me. "Girls," she says, "come on! Time to pack up. Time to go home."

"Just one more swim," Daisy begs, just like she always does. Mom nods and smiles, just like she always does.

"Just one more, Daddy, throw me!"

Laughing, Danny gets up, runs back into the water, scoops Daisy up and she leaps, shrieking, into the waves.

He doesn't throw me into the waves. I'm too big for that, he says.

I run into the water too. Then I dive, loving the soft shimmery coolness.

I swim and swim and swim.

......

"Morley. Morley darling, it's me. It's Mum. Morley, sweetheart, say something. Can you hear me?"

Of course I can hear her.

"Yes. I hear you," I say. But what comes out is more like mumble-croak-mumble. My mouth tastes like sick and my whole head hurts and I don't want to talk to anyone.

Then someone puts their hand on my head. It's an old man in a white coat. He smells funny. He gets too close to me. He tries to shine a little flash-light into my eyes. I pull away from him, because he's hurting me. He's holding my shoulders now, and I gag.

"She's going to be a bit groggy," the man says, as if I'm not even there. "Bump on the head. Affects the memory. These things take time, Mrs., uh, Ms..."

"Star," my mother says.

"And patience," the man says, ignoring her.

"Morley," my mother says again. Then, more loudly, as if my ears aren't working, "MORLEY. Wake up darling. Please. Just wake up. For Mummy." Now she's almost on top of me, trying to hug me, which hurts so I try to get away.

"I AM awake," I say. I think I'm shouting, but it comes out as a sort of grunty whisper.

Suddenly, the hugging stops and I gasp for breath.

"Morley. Sweetheart. I'm so sorry..." My mom is apologizing. To me.

This is so weird I definitely want to know what's going

31

on.

My mother has a LOT of rules in our house, all of which seem to be for me and hardly any of them for my sister. This is because, Mum says, "she's still little." When things go wrong...well, let's just say the one who ends up having to do the apologizing is just about always me. Sorry Morley. That could be my real name.

But now, it's what my mother is saying.

To me.

And anyone else who is in this room, whoever they are. Wherever this is.

"I'm so sorry..." she says. "Morley. Sweetheart."

She is?

Sorry?

For what?

Strangely enough, I don't really care, because just now, I feel like I am sort of floating.

The floating me knows about the pain, but she doesn't care. It just doesn't matter.

The man says something to the nurse, who follows him out of the room. My mother stays behind. Sniffling into a tissue.

Then doing something with her phone.

Another nurse comes in, nods to my mother, and puts a bag full of clear stuff that looks like water on a hook next to the bed.

My mother sits on a chair next to the bed.

She's crying.

I don't know why.

I don't see Daisy anywhere. Or Danny. Or anyone else I know.

I know that the girl in the bed is me, but I don't care very much. The girl has a terrible sick headache and her right arm is in some kind of white tube. Someone says that something is wrong with her ribs, which is why she can't breathe very good.

Under the pajamas and the white sheet and the skimpy white blanket, this girl has a whole lot of new bruises on her front and her legs. Along with, of course, all the old bruises.

The ones that nobody knows about, except maybe Jayden and Sam.

I don't know how I know this.

What's really odd is I know that girl in the white room bed is me. She got hurt somehow.

She needs to sleep, because sleep time is when you heal. That hurting will stop when the healing works.

But the strange thing is, it doesn't really matter.

And I'm sorry my Mum is crying and it looks like it's my fault, but there's nothing I can do about it.

I want to sleep. And sleep and sleep, for a long time. Maybe forever and ever.

Then, I'm floating on my back in the ocean. On a

summer afternoon.

Looking up at the sky. Watching the seagulls drifting above. Just floating and drifting.

Drifting and floating on an endless blue sky.

And dreaming...

......

"Morley."

A woman's voice.

Not the nurse.

Not my mother.

Not anyone I know.

"Morley. Are you awake?"

I don't want to be. But I open my eyes. I hope this woman brought some food. A fruit smoothie. And some chicken nuggets. Or pizza with extra cheese. That would be good. I'm really hungry.

"Morley!"

It is a woman, but she isn't holding anything to eat. She has a police officer uniform on.

"Morley," she says. "I'm Linda and this is Carol." She points at another woman who's old like my teacher, Mrs. Green. Same pinched look on her face, like there's a bad smell in the room. Same wispy brown hair with gray roots.

"We need to talk to you about what happened. About who hurt you. Who's hurting you."

"Oh?" I say. Or try to. "Why?"

"Who hurt you, Morley?"

Daisy, I think. And Julia. I don't say anything.

"What do you remember about what happened?"

I try to think. What do I remember? A drawing. I was doing a drawing. Of Jayden. And Spirit.

That's what I say.

I talk very slowly, because it hurts to get enough air to talk. I grab little bits of air and say a few words and then do it again. And again.

My voice doesn't sound like me at all. But the woman, the one who says her name is Linda, just waits. The other woman, what did she say her name is? She writes something in a black binder. I like it that she doesn't interrupt.

"OK. Good. You were at home. Drawing a picture. For your friend. Then what did you do?"

"Um...outside. Went. Outside."

"Yes. Why did you do that? Where were you going?"

I try to remember.

"Outside," I say. "Raining."

"When?"

"Today?"

"What do you mean?" the other woman, the one in the

baggy sweater, says.

"Today?" I gasp, my chest hurting. "Outside. Today?"

"Today is Monday," the police woman says. "It wasn't today."

That can't be right.

"Happy. Friday," I say. "Cel. Ebrate…"

"It's the painkillers," a man's voice says then. "And she's had quite a knock on the head. It's going to take some time for her to remember…and right now, you're tiring her, so time's up, I'm afraid…"

But right then my mother is in the room, and she's yelling, louder than I've ever heard her. "WHAT ARE YOU PEOPLE DOING?" she shrieks, grabbing the police officer by the arm. "GET AWAY FROM MY DAUGHTER!"

And then everything is just a noisy mess with people shouting, and other people telling them to CALM DOWN and BE SENSIBLE and then some other men that look like guards arrive and everybody goes out in the hallway.

Except me.

But they leave the door a little bit open and I can hear bits of what they're saying. Especially my mother, because she's the loudest.

It almost makes me want to laugh, because she sounds just like Daisy. A grown-up Daisy who's even louder. And madder.

"You can't!" my mother shrieks. "I won't let you! You have no right to…"

"Concussion," the man says. I think he must be a doctor. "...memories filter back..."

There are other women's voices, but they're quieter. I can't quite make out what they're saying. I don't know who says what. Some of the words I can hear are "over-react," "protect children," "co-operate with us, Ms. Star" and "the old bruises."

What's happening out in the hallway is all a jumble. Then, suddenly, it's quiet, as if everyone has gone away.

I'm alone.

What do I remember? I try to make my brain work.

Something about supper.

And Daisy.

Rain.

Cold.

Hard.

Pain.

Can't move.

Can't breathe.

Pain.

......

Then it's another time and maybe even another day.

I'm awake and sort of sitting up and I have a tray of food in front of me.

Nothing I like. A box of orange-mango juice. A plastic bowl of oatmeal with brown bits in it. White bread. Little plastic things of jam and honey that you need two hands to open. An orange. I push it away.

"Eat something," my mother says. "Just try."

I try to eat the oatmeal with the spoon in my left hand, because my right hand and arm are in a cast. It hurts and the cast feels too tight. My arm must be broken.

"It's your wrist," Mom says. "But it's healing now."

Eating is just too hard. I give up. The oatmeal tastes like wet cardboard anyways.

The baggy-sweater woman is back and she's saying, "We'll be looking at the home situation, Ms. Star. About why your daughter has these injuries. The recent ones and the older ones. The bruises. Because we have to be sure..."

My mother just sits there, ignoring her.

"Children must be protected. Surely you understand? You work with children, don't you, Ms. Star? In your job?"

I think there's going to be another fight. Instead, my mother turns her back to the woman. She starts peeling the orange from my food tray, handing me orange slices I don't want.

"A home assessment," the woman says.

I try to remember what *assessment* means. Isn't that something like *understanding*? Home understanding?

What could that be?

"And in the meantime, we think it's best that your other daughter stays with relatives. Just while we..."

"WHAT?" My mother says, turning so suddenly she knocks over the glass of water on my tray and it drips on the blanket. "You can't take Daisy away from me..."

"Just until we know for sure, Ms. Star. We'll say Thursday...at 10? We'll need you to be there...and the father?"

What father, I'm wondering. Does she mean Daisy's father? But Danny is away in the city. Working.

"Won't be there," my mother tells the woman. "Not in the picture. Never has been."

What picture is she talking about? Later, when I ask her, she just shrugs.

"We're fine, Morley," my mother says. "You're going to be fine. It was just an accident."

An accident.

Some kind of accident. A car accident?

I was in some kind of accident.

"What accident?" I say. "When?"

"You went outside to call Daisy. Something happened. I don't know what, exactly. But you both fell. Daisy was very brave. She was hurt too, but she got up and ran to get me and I called 9-1-1 and then the ambulance came, you remember…"

I fell? We fell? But that's so strange. It wasn't snowing, or icy out or anything. Why would we fall? How could it be bad enough to have to go to hospital?

None of it makes sense.

After my mother has gone home, after the nurse said it was time to sleep, after they turned the lights down but not off so the room still has spooky light and I'm just lying there staring at the shadows on the walls, I try to think about all this.

And what it could mean.

Finally, I give up.

What I really want is for Sam and Jayden to come and visit. Maybe they know what happened. And why.

Maybe they could bring something good to eat.

But kids aren't allowed to visit. It's a hospital rule.

So, no Daisy visit, which is OK with me. I don't think I could stand all the noise she makes right now. But also, no Sam and no Jayden, which makes me feel alone and sad.

I really miss my two best friends.

three

It's almost three weeks later and I'm so totally bored, I'm wishing I was back at school.

Almost.

I'm propped up with cushions on our living room couch, talking to Sam and Jayden.

Sam is the smartest girl in our class. Jayden is a boy in the other grade 5. We hang out most school days at lunch and we have art class and language class together. We've been best friends since grade 2.

They come over to visit almost every day after school. We've already talked about how Daisy jumped out of the apple tree. That's what happened. It took a while, but slowly I started to remember that day.

Or sort of remember. Some of it, people told me. Like about the ambulance coming and dinner getting cold on the stove and mum forgetting to lock the front door and Daisy crying.

And mom and Daisy waiting in the hospital.

And Daisy falling asleep on a chair until mom took her home.

Daisy wasn't hurt. Not really. All she got was a few bruises and a couple of scratches. She hardly even needed a band-aid.

What I got, when she landed on top of me, was two cracked ribs, a broken wrist, a cut on my forehead that needed eight stitches and a lot of bruises.

It's a lot easier to breathe than it was. I only had to stay in hospital for five days. That's the good news.

Those stitches looked like fat ants crawling across my face, so I guess it's more good news that they're gone. Now there's just a reddish-pink line where the stitches were. Mom rubs this special oil on my forehead every morning and again just before bedtime. It's supposed to make the scar fade away.

Today, I also got another arm x-ray and another new cast and it's also good news that my wrist isn't throbbing all the time like it was. Though it's still weak. Too weak to let me draw or paint very much yet.

I have to do these special exercises to get my right hand and arm strong again. They aren't much fun.

Ribs heal themselves, Dr. Carolyn said. It will take about two months for my wrist to heal completely and not that long for everything else except the scar on my face. It will fade. Eventually.

Eventually means some time in the future. I don't know how long in the future.

But it already feels like it's been a long, long time, like it was weeks and weeks ago that it happened. The accident.

I don't think it was an accident. That's just what mom calls it.

I'm still angry with Daisy, because it was all her stupid fault. And she never apologized until mom made her.

My mother was angry with me, because she says all I was supposed to do was go call my sister for supper and we ended up at the hospital and I gave her the fright of her life and *what was I thinking*?

And aren't I the older sister, supposed to be the sensible one? The one that doesn't cause her all this grief?

Not to mention how embarrassed she was about the home assessment. That turned out to be a report to see if she is a good parent and we have a good home and I didn't get hurt because someone in our family is hurting me on purpose.

I hated the way the police woman and that other woman kept on asking me about what it's like at our house, and do people ever get angry? And then what happens? And does my mother hit me? Or my stepfather?

And I also felt really angry with my mother, because it felt like she was blaming me for the whole thing. And she wasn't the one who ended up with stitches and a cast on her arm and a body that hurts.

So how was it my fault?

Why do I always have to be the smart one and the sensible one? What if I want to be the pretty one, or the creative one, or even the dare-devil one?

Or none of these. What if I don't want to be the anything one, I just want to be me, Morley Jane Elizabeth Star?

Just – ME.

Exactly the way I AM.

I asked mom this, but she just said, "Oh, Morley, really..." and went back to the kitchen.

She doesn't want to talk about it. No one does, except Sam and Jayden.

I'm not angry at everyone. Not my friends. Not my Aunt Eira, who's been really kind. She comes over every morning to be with me while my mum's at work. She's who Daisy stayed with, until the police woman and that other woman let Daisy come home.

"You've got a lot to be happy about," Doctor Carolyn says. If that's true, maybe SHE should have had the accident or whatever it was, so SHE could have stitches and a cast and everything hurting and be all happy about it. "You're healing nicely. It's fine for you to go back to school in another week or so. When you feel ready. Maybe half-days to start. Build up your strength."

I could tell that mom is glad to hear this. She's been

home with me a lot, even though I told her I'm old enough to be home alone. Almost.

At first, she tried to keep me company, playing Crazy 8s or Monopoly or Chinese checkers, but everything just felt too hard to do. Finally, she mostly left me alone with the remote.

While she did more baking.

For once, I don't care. And I get to eat some of it. Though eating is one of the hard things now.

It's surprising what you can't do when you're ache-y all over and the hand you always use isn't working and you have a big hunk of plaster cast on your arm. And you still feel kinda dizzy.

Of course, you still know how to use a spoon or knife and fork, or get dressed, or brush your teeth, or any of those things you learn to do when you're little. But it's just *harder* to do any of these things by using the 'wrong' hand. And everything takes so much longer.

If you don't think using the wrong hand matters much, you should try writing, or eating, or brushing your teeth, or getting dressed or anything you normally do, but do it only by using your 'other' hand, the one you don't always use. This means if you're right-handed, like me, try doing everything with only your left hand.

It's crazy how tricky it is!

And it's really embarrassing, having to ask your aunt or your mother to help you, like you're a big baby.

When you have a cast, you can't take a bath. You

have to just take showers, with a plastic bag on over the cast.

You also can't go in the pool, so I have to miss swimming lessons. And that's one of my favourite things.

I've tried writing with my left hand, just to see what happens. My left hand can't draw at all, but it can print, sort of. It looks like a scrawl, like what little kids do in Grade 1.

It's really hard to hold books open with just one hand, and there's no way to hold a book and turn the pages, so I gave up on reading. I've watched every movie we have at least three times. Playing video games with only one hand is just too difficult.

I wish I could be drawing, but my wrist throbs when I try to hold a pencil or marker. So, I can't finish that drawing of Jayden and Spirit, the one I was making for his birthday present.

I missed Jayden's birthday party. It happened while I was in hospital. I know my mum bought a card and a gift certificate and gave them to Jayden from me, but it's not the same.

You might think it would be great to get off school and just laze around while all the other kids have to work. But even with my friends visiting every day...

...even with my mother here and trying not to be annoyed with me even though she wants what she calls "everything back to normal"...

...even with all this "relaxing" I'm doing...

...even with Daisy at kindergarten every morning and at daycare every afternoon so I get some peace, I'm just SO tired of hanging around with nothing to do but worry about things like when Danny is coming back. How I'll get a pet. Why those renters don't move some place else.

Wishing I could feel like myself again.

BE myself again.

Just me. Morley. A girl in grade 5 who likes to draw and do crafts and lives in a little town near the ocean with her mother and her annoying little sister and Danny. And a pet cat or dog.

And they're all happy.

Together.

......

On another afternoon, Sam and Jayden are at my house. Too soon, they get ready to leave. Sam, because she has to practice her violin. Jayden, because he has chores. He's the youngest kid in their family, but he says on a farm, everyone works.

Mom is buzzing around, bringing us lemonade and asking if anyone wants more cookies. The kitchen counter is overflowing with baked goods. I expect mom will send my friends home with bags of goodies.

They always come with gifts. Art supplies, which I'm excited to use as soon as my wrist gets stronger. Craft kits to make beaded necklaces or friendship bracelets. Video games. Audio books, and Jayden's lent me his audio player and showed me how to use it, so I can listen to music. Cherries, my favorite fruit, all the way from California. And Sam brought her new puppy to visit. She's called Tippy.

Tippy is too squirmy to sit on my lap. She bounces around the room and does silly stuff and we all laugh. For once, mom doesn't seem to mind that there's a pet in our house. Of all the treats and gifts that people have given me, having Tippy over is the best. Even though laughing still makes my ribs hurt.

"Tell me about your birthday party," I say.

Sam loves to talk about any kind of celebration. She's an only child, so her parties are epic.

I can't go this year, because the rule is no swimming until the cast comes off. And what use is it, going to a pool party and just sitting there, watching all the other kids splashing around and having fun?

Jayden pats my shoulder. "Come on, cheer up. You'll still get to swim this summer!"

"And besides," Sam says, "Here's some news. It's not going to be *just* a pool party this year. It's going to be even more EPIC!"

"WHAT?" Jayden and I both say at the same time and we all laugh. "What kind of epic?"

"It's a surprise," Sam says, reaching for another cookie.

"Oh come on," we beg. "You can tell us. It can be our

secret. Promise!"

"Nope," Sam says. "You'll just have to wait to find out!"

In the end, we talk her into giving us just one hint about her party. Here it is: "It has something to do with something in the living room right now that you got as a get-well gift."

Jayden and I both beg for more, but that's all Sam will say.

Something in the room that was a gift, I'm thinking after they leave. It can't be the homework from Mrs. Green...or the movies Jayden brought over...or the paper airplane folding kit Sam brought. So, well, what?

And then I know the answer, and I can't stop smiling.

It's about Tippy's visit. And that means...a PETS party.

I can hardly wait!

four

Aunt Eira is mom's youngest sister. Our other aunt, Aunt Sorcha, was the middle kid in their family. Mom is the oldest.

I love it when Aunt Eira comes over to keep me company.

Sometimes we talk. One day, I ask her about what it was like, when she was growing up?

She tells me about how their family lived on a farm and had lots of animals. How my grandparents also ran a little store, selling baking and eggs and milk and most of the stuff you find in convenience stores now. How she always thought mom was being bossy, but really, she was a good older sister.

"And really funny, Morley. Always telling jokes! Like your Aunt Sorcha."

So not much like mom now, I think.

"And good at just about everything she wanted to do. I always thought...well, I thought she'd be a teacher."

"Is that what she wanted to be?"

"It was. Yes. Until...well, until the ba...until she was a teenager and other things happened."

I wondered what other things. But now she's talking about our grandfather, who's retired. We don't see him very often.

"Why did Danny leave?" I ask.

"Well, you know he lost his job here, and..." I know that. Kids at school said he got fired because he's a dirty rotten thief and he stole money from the car company where he worked. Then the police came and arrested him and threw him in jail. And that's why he can't come home.

I think that's all a lie, but no one will tell me what really happened.

"Is that the real reason?"

"Oh Morley. You really have to ask your mother..."

"He doesn't want to be in our family any more, does he?"

Aunt Eira looks at her hands, pushing back a cuticle on one of her nails. She doesn't look at me.

"Is it because he doesn't like us any more?"

"Oh Morley," my aunt says. "I don't know. If you ask your mother..."

"I did. She won't tell me anything."

"I'm sorry, sweetheart. Except I know it isn't about you or Daisy. Your mother and Danny care very much about both of you. It's just sometimes...adults...well, it's about them."

"Are they getting a divorce?" This is the question I've worried about. The one I didn't want to ask.

"Sort of."

"What do you mean? I don't understand."

"Me either. But I think it's just that they don't want to be together any more. But they want good things for you and Daisy. They want you to be happy."

We *were* happy. We were a family. Together.

But what if Danny didn't want that any more? Is that why he left?

Or did he have to leave?

Or maybe my mother made him leave. Maybe she was the one who didn't want to be a family any more.

"If a person doesn't want to be in your family, can you make them be?" Can you get them back, somehow? Can you make them change their mind? Can you do something – anything – to put your family together again?

"You can't make other people do anything, Morley," my aunt says, leaning forward to hug me very gently. "People do what they want to do or need to do for their lives. For what matters the most to them. And who they are.

"Your family is everyone who wants to be yours. And you want to be theirs. Like you and me. And your mom. And Daisy. And your Aunt Sorcha. And your grandpa. We'll always be your family. And you'll be our family, because we all love you." She kisses me on the top of the head and says, "You know, Morley, families change, sometimes."

"Even when they love each other."

"Even then. Especially then."

And then she leaves me to think about all this while she heads back to her laptop to work.

Aunt Eira has her own business. She went to college and got a degree from Business School. Now she has a blog and sells things online. Sometimes she shows me stuff about using computers, like how to find a song you want to hear on YouTube or put pictures of things you really like on Pinterest.

I think about what she said. Families love you. Families change.

I want our family to be exactly the way it was. And it will be, when Danny comes back.

And my mother finally says we can have a pet.

That's every single thing I hope for.

......

Another afternoon, Eira is working on her laptop and I'm flipping through the channels and come to this show called *Daytime with Lorraine*.

Lorraine talks like she comes from Scotland. I have to listen really closely to understand her. Sometimes, she has famous people on her show to talk about stuff. Generally, I'd just flip away, because the stuff they talk about is boring, like how to make good school lunches or clever ways to tie scarves.

But today, Lorraine says they have a special craft coming up, right after the break. "We're making Wish Bracelets!" she says, like that's the most exciting thing she's ever done in her entire life. "So stay with us!"

Then there's an advertisement for a car that is easy to drive fast when there are rocks falling off a cliff and one for potato chips, and a new kind of shampoo and a yogurt that helps you exercise and a few more, but I'm not paying attention. Finally, Lorraine is back and now she's sitting at a little table, next to another woman, or maybe she's a teenager because she looks really young. But not a kid.

Lorraine says that this is Alleeza Ahmed, and she makes jewellery and sells it in boutiques and online. Alleeza is going to show us how to make a Wish Bracelet.

"So, what's that?" Lorraine asks. "Is it like a friendship bracelet?"

"Yes," Alleeza says. She's got long dark hair and she's smiling. She has a lot of bracelets on. She points to three of them and says, "These are all wish bracelets. They're really fast and easy to make. And a nice gift!"

I like her. I think it would be cool to know her. And I like the bracelets, so I keep watching.

"And what do you need to make them?" Lorraine has a lot of bracelets on, too. Hers are the metal kind. They clank when she moves her arms, which she does a lot. She talks with her whole body. It's like she almost can't sit still.

"Simple. Just some hemp string and a few beads, any colours you want," Alleeza says. "Then you'll need scissors. I use a beading board, like this..." and she holds up something that looks like a piece of cardboard, but it's green and it has markings on it. "...but you don't really need one. You can find everything you need at the craft store. Or a good dollar store. Or buy it online."

"Lovely," Lorraine says, picking through all the little containers of beads. "So, you're going to show me how to make my own Wish Bracelet in just five minutes?"

"Right. Cut three pieces of your string, about this long. Hold the three together at one end. Start with a knot, like this," Alleeza says. "Then all you do is braid, for about two inches. Or five centimetres."

She measures the braiding she's done. "Now, you want to add your beads. What colour?"

"Oh, I'll take red," Lorraine says. "I'm a red kind of girl!"

"Red it is," Alleeza says, adding a bead, snuggling it into place, then another until there are five beads in a row. Then she does more braiding and, in just a minute or two, she's done. The camera zooms in to show the finished bracelet.

While she's doing all this, they're talking. "So how did you get this idea for a Wish Bracelet, Alleeza?"

"It wasn't entirely my idea. I remember my gran doing them, long ago, on rainy days. She showed my sister and me how. So you make a wish when you put on your bracelet. You keep it on all the time. When the hemp string breaks, all the beads scatter."

"And your wish bracelet is gone."

"Yes, it is. But then, your wish comes true. So what will you wish for?"

Lorraine just smiles. "We have to take a break now, but stay with us to find out..."

But I'm no longer listening.

Your wish comes true.

That's what makes it so cool. It's not just something pretty to wear. The bracelet breaks and your wish comes true.

I wonder if it works? Or is it more like reading your horoscope, which is kinda true, sometimes?

I need to know.

I rummage around in our crafts closet and in the friendship bracelets kit Sam gave me for a get-well gift and find everything I need.

That afternoon, I make two wish bracelets. It's a lot easier to braid and put on beads and tie knots than it is to draw. Even with a cast.

My right hand gets tired, so I stop and rest a lot. Then start up again.

I know what I'll wish for.

The one with reddish-amber beads is about our family. As I make it, I think of my wish that, really soon, Danny comes home so my mum can be happy and we can be a normal family again, with a father, a mother and two kids. That's Daisy and me.

And some pets.

My second wish bracelet with golden yellow beads is also about family. It's for my new pet cat.

I hope they both break, like tomorrow. Or really soon. But making them break is probably cheating. It might stop the magic from happening.

So I just have to put them on and wait and see what happens.

But, with a cast on, I can't put them on and tie the strings. I need help.

By the time Jayden and Sam arrive after school, I've made the two wish bracelets for me, and one for each of them. And one for my mother. And one for Daisy.

Jayden's has purple beads. Sam's has beads that are jade green. Their favourite colours. I wonder what their wishes will be.

We put them on when we're together. And each make our own wishes.

And promise to tell each other.

When our secret wishes come true.

five

On the last day before I go back to school, Sam and Jayden are over at my house, just hanging out. And playing with Tippy.

"So why can't you have a pet?" Sam says. "The real reason?"

"Don't know," I say. "Mom won't even talk about it. She just says we've got a No Pets Rule. But that can't be true, because the renters have a cat."

"For real?" Jayden says. "How do you know?"

Because I hear it. All the time. But they'll think that bump I got on the head has made me crazy, so I don't tell them that. "I saw it once," I say, telling a lie but it's just a little lie. "In the upstairs window. Trying to get out on the balcony."

"So the people upstairs can have a cat, but you can't?

That's not fair!" Sam says.

"Maybe." Jayden reaches for another cookie. "But I think it doesn't matter."

"It doesn't matter?" Sam says, as if this is one of the stupidest things she's ever heard. "How can you say that?"

"Well, because there must be a reason you don't know about. And..." he takes another swallow of milk. "...Instead of just getting sad about it, or mad about it, I think you could change it."

"Change what my mom says?" I ask. As if that will ever happen. She's already said, "NO!" like a thousand times.

"Change how you're asking," Jayden says.

"You think if I just ask nicely, suddenly she'll say, "Yes?"

"As if," Sam says. "That would NEVER work with my mother!"

"So what do you guys know about cats?"

"Not much," Sam says, giving Tippy the last of her oatmeal cookie. "I've never had one."

"There's four types of cats," Jayden says.

"You mean like long-hair and short-hair and those really weird ones that are totally bald?"

"Or like black, or ginger, or gray, or all different colours?" Sam says.

"Um, no," he says. "I mean wild cats, barn cats,

outdoor cats and indoor cats."

"Wild cats? Like lions and tigers?" Sam says, teasing him.

"Feral cats," Jayden says, ignoring her. "They might be pets that don't have a home and try to live on their own. Or they never had a home.

"They live outside and try to survive. So that's one, the cats that are feral. Then there's barn cats. They have a job to do, keeping the mice and rats away from the feed for the farm animals. In return, they get lots to eat and a safe, warm place to sleep. If they're lucky.

"Number three is pet cats that live inside but also go outside. They hunt for birds and mice, but sometimes they like to live indoors, with people."

"And the last type is totally indoor cats?"

Jayden smiles and nods. "They're the luckiest, because they're the healthiest and they can live the longest."

"Why?" Sam and I say at the same time.

"Because they get good care from their owners. They're protected from the dangers of being outside, like being attacked by another animal or hit by a car. They get fresh water and enough food. And they get taken to the vet and get their shots and get spayed or neutered."

"What's that?"

"Oh, I know," Sam says. "Shots are to not get sick, so they don't get heartworm or distemper or cancer, kind of like when we get shots so we don't get measles or the flu."

"Ick – worms, in their heart? Really?"

"Really. Dogs get it," Sam says.

"And what was that other word? Sprayed?"

"Spayed. It means making it so your pet won't ever have babies."

"But that would be so much fun!" Sam says.

"It would. But also, you couldn't keep them all. You'd have to find homes for them, and..."

Sam finishes his sentence. "And there's already a lot of pets who need homes. At the pet shelters."

Jayden nods. "But also a lot of people who want a pet and come to adopt them. The lucky ones."

I finger the beads on my wish bracelet with the yellow beads and think about how I could be one of those lucky ones.

Sam says what I'm thinking. "So how could Morley get to adopt the cat she wants? From the pet shelter. When her mom keeps saying, "No!"

"I have an idea..." Jayden says. "I think you're going to like it!"

six

"I think what we need is a plan," Jayden says.

"A plan?" I ask. "What for?"

"You mean, like how you plan your birthday party?" Sam asks. Her party's still weeks away, but it is Very Important to her. She loves talking about it.

"Something like that. Only this is the Get A Pet Plan," Jayden says. "But, yeah, basically the same."

"Basically how?" I ask, wondering how getting your birthday party organized is like getting a pet when your mother just keeps saying "NO pets!"

"Here's what I'm thinking," Jayden says, as if he's thinking out loud. "If you keep asking your mom the same way, she's going to keep answering the same way. Right?"

"Um, yeah. I guess," I say, wondering what he's going

to say next.

"So, to get a different answer, the answer you want, maybe something has to change."

"Well, duh," I say. "Of course. She has to change what she says."

"Or you do."

Sam looks as confused as I am.

"You mean I have to stop asking for a pet?"

"Nope. You have to ask differently. Ask better."

"I don't understand..." I say. How many ways can there be to ask for something? Don't you just – ask?

"Well, like at Christmas time. Or when it's your birthday and you really, really want something. Do you just ask for it?

"Sure..." I say. Why wouldn't you just ask for something you want or need?

"Well, not exactly..." Sam says.

I stare at them both in disbelief. Change how you ask for things and you might get them? I've never, ever thought this before. Could it be possible? Would it work? How?

But before I can ask, Jayden says, "You need a plan, not just asking. Like doing a project. Or a piece of art. You don't do it all at once, do you?"

"Well, no..."

"There are steps to get started, keep going and then finish, right?"

"Yeah. Right. But..."

"But getting a pet is the same. There are steps to get ready to have a pet."

"But I don't know what they are..." I say.

"Because you don't have a pet. But Sam and I do. So why don't we help you get your pet?"

And then I think yeah, why not? And I also think I'm so lucky to have Jayden and Sam as my best friends.

"Have you got a big sheet of paper? Or a roll of newsprint? Or poster board?" Jayden says.

We do. In the craft closet. Soon, we've got a big page spread out on the coffee table, with a pile of coloured markers scattered around.

"So, how do we start?"

"We start with a total brain dump. Anything about having a pet. Everything you can think of. Just write it down. Anywhere on the page. In any colour you want."

"There's no right way to do it?" Sam asks.

"Any way you want is the right way," Jayden says.

Then we all start writing. Here are some of the things we write on the poster:

Pets are good for kids.

Pets cost money.

Cats shed hair all over.

Cats smell, especially the litter box.

They need to go to the vet.

You need to brush their fur and be sure their eyes and ears are clean.

You need to clip their claws.

You should brush their teeth.

"What?" I say when Jayden writes this down. "Brush their teeth? Are you crazy?"

"Don't stop to think about it – just keep going. That's important." Jayden says.

Finally, when there's writing all over the poster, we run out of things to add.

Then we start drawing in arrows between things that go together.

Jayden says what we've got now is a map. He calls it a mind map. He says they learned this in his grade 5 from their teacher, Mr. Cadeau. They broke up into teams with four kids in each team. Then they picked their project.

Jayden's team decided they would design the perfect professional car racing team. They would be the team manager and say who they'd have on their team, and why. They worked on the racing strategy for the next season, so they'd have a chance to win the Formula 1 championship.

Jayden said that in their class, their projects had four things to do. Number one is brain storming your mind map, which is writing everything you can think of down. Really fast. And not stopping to talk about if it was good or bad, just get every single thought down on paper.

Step Two, he said, is to look at everything you wrote down, and start connecting things. Then make a plan about what work there is to do and who will do it.

Step Three is to get that work done!

Step Four is to present your project. And celebrate getting it done and being a success!

So, we do a mind map for getting a pet. And all the reasons my mom has not to.

Then we turn the poster paper over, and start writing down all the ways to find out about pets. We do this so we can have the right answers to all the questions and reasons mom has. Like what kinds of pets don't shed very much hair. And how much it really costs to have a pet. And lots more questions like that.

To find the answers, we could read books from the library. Or search online – I know my Aunt Eira would help me do this. Or Jayden's brother Patrick. Or I could talk to people who have pets and know this stuff, or a lot of it.

Then we think of all the ways to put everything we learn about pets together. "You could do a report," Jayden says.

"Or a video for YouTube," Sam says. "Or give a speech. Or a presentation. Ask your mother to watch it."

"Or write a book for kids, maybe a graphic novel with your drawings. Or create a pets trivia game, or…"

"OK, I get it. But that sounds like a lot of work," I say,

suddenly feeling tired just thinking about it.

"But if it helps you get your pet," Jayden says. "Isn't it going to be worth it? That is, if it's what you *really* want. Badly enough to work hard to get it?"

Yes, it is what I really want. And that's the day the Get A Pet project gets started.

We borrow books about pets from the library at school and the one in town.

Aunt Eira and Jayden's brother Patrick help me look online and find out how much it costs to adopt a cat from the pet shelter. And what other things do you need to buy for your pet?

Jayden's mom tells us about what shots kittens and puppies need, and about other things like why you should brush their teeth with special pet toothpaste. It's because they can get cavities in their teeth that really hurt, just like people get.

Cavities can get so bad if you don't go to the dentist (or the vet, for pets) that the poison cavities create can make you really, really sick. Maybe even kill you, if the infection gets bad enough. That's also true for pets.

I never knew that. I never would have guessed, if we weren't doing the Get A Pet project.

We learned that in some towns and cities, you need to buy a license to have a dog. But there aren't licenses for cats.

We learned that there's different types of food. Cats can only eat meat. Dogs can eat just about everything people eat, except chocolate. They like it, but it's a poison, if you're a dog. Or a cat.

And I also learned all the ways to solve the problems my mom has about pets. They don't smell when you keep them, their bed and their litter box clean.

They shed less if you brush their fur with a special pet brush.

They don't take up very much space, especially cats.

Cats are safer, healthier and they live longer if they're indoor cats. Even though that seems mean, making them stay inside all the time when they love to be outside, it's better.

Outside cats kill songbirds and most songbirds are vanishing or they're already endangered.

Cats like their ears scratched, gently. They don't like to be picked up. They do like to sit on your lap, when they feel like it. They don't usually like car rides, or baths, or people touching their paws. They do like climbing up to high places and looking down on their world. They like routines and staying home.

You have to be careful about choosing your pet, because they can live a long time. 10 or 15 years for a dog, sometimes longer. 20 years, or more, for an inside cat that gets good care.

I found out that pets who claw furniture or destroy things are probably lonely or bored. Cats need a scratching post of their own. All pets need toys and play time with their humans. Just like little kids.

I work on the Get A Pet plan just about every day.

Sam and Jayden help sometimes.

And while I'd doing the pet plan, I have two thoughts. One is that with Danny gone, I know my mom doesn't have a lot of money. And pets cost money. Part of my plan has to say how to pay for my pet. I need an earn-some-money plan as well.

And maybe I need a third plan. Because, after all, the other wish bracelet might need some help from me. I need a Get Danny Home plan.

I pull out another poster board, my markers, and do the mind map for that.

seven

On my first day back to school, Mrs. Green makes a big fuss about "welcoming" me to our grade 5 classroom, as if I'd never been there before. I was hoping nobody would know what happened. Maybe I could just say I had the flu or something. But it seems like everyone in my class already knows. If not, Mrs. Green makes sure they do.

Some kids want to sign my cast.

Some have questions, like what does my arm feel like? The answer is sore, but mainly itchy.

Is it ever going to work right? Yes. But I have to do special exercises to make it strong again.

Don't I miss using my hand? Yes, but that weird tingly feeling is gone. I can use it a little bit already.

Most kids don't care much and I'm happier not having

to keep talking about it.

And some kids want me to make them a wish bracelet, like the ones I made for Jayden and Sam. "Sure," I say, "I can do that. They're $2 each. What colour beads do you want?" Then I write down what they ask for. Kids pay me $12 the first week I'm back at school for making them wish bracelets.

Mrs. Green says I can stay inside during recess, if I need a rest. Also, I can sit out gym class, which is my second-worst subject. So that's what I do.

At lunch, I'm not very hungry, so I give my meatloaf sandwich and cookies to Jayden, who is tall and skinny and a food vacuum cleaner.

Sam offers me half of her granola bar. "Are you glad you're back?"

I'm about to say sort of, at least it's better than lying around all the time thinking about what hurts, when Jayden spots Julia and her usual followers coming our way.

"Don't look now, but here comes the Wicked Witch of Fifth Grade," Jayden says. "But the bell's gonna go off. We should go."

"Hey Sorry-Morry!" Julia shouts, scowling in my direction. "Heard you got tromped on and went all looney tunes cuz your brain got smashed!"

"Just ignore her," Sam whispers. "Maybe she'll go away."

"Forget that," Jayden says. "Let's go. It's time for the bell anyway."

Julia is right in front of me now, almost on top of me, with Crystal and Tiffany, her Mean Girl gang, standing right behind her. "Yeah, I heard it was your crazy sister who jumped on you. That must have been really funny!"

"Oh, shut up, Julia!" Jayden says. "You don't know anything. Come on, Morley!"

Julia ignores him. "Real funny, I said!" Julia does her fake-y laugh and pokes me hard on my right arm. "Wish I'd been there, I wouldn't have stopped laughing, HA HA! You're so dumb, you didn't even get out of the way!"

"You don't know anything about what happened," I shout at Julia. "You don't know anything at all!" Then I duck around her and run to catch up with the other kids, even though it hurts to run, knowing Julia is right behind me.

My heart is pumping so hard, I wonder if I'm having a heart attack. I feel dizzy when I get to my seat.

I'm trying to listen to Mrs. Green talking about the ocean tides and how they're caused by the moon, which sounds kind of silly because how can the moon move water around? But my mind just drifts away.

Maybe, for once, bully Julia is right about something. Maybe I shouldn't have tried to catch Daisy.

If I hadn't, she might have been hurt, instead of me. Or maybe, with her usual Daisy-luck, she'd hardly be hurt at all. A bruise or two, that's all.

But there wasn't any time to stop and think, when it happened.

It just happened.

Suddenly, it feels like it's happening all over again. I shout something to Daisy. I look up. She's in the air and she's just stuck there, arms and legs spread out, laughing.

It's like she's a picture of Daisy, glued to the sky high above my head.

And then I'm on the ground, and it's hard and cold. I'm trying to get up, but it hurts so bad.

And then mom is there, trying to lift me up. And the pain is so bad, I can't see.

And then I don't remember anything until we get to the hospital and there are people rushing around, lifting me up, pulling off my clothes. And then it's later, and I'm waking up, with my mother there.

It just happened. An accident, everyone says, even though I know Daisy jumped on purpose.

I'm still trying to figure out how I feel about what happened. And about my sister.

eight

Usually I get up early on Saturday mornings.

I pour cereal and milk for Daisy and make toast for me and get us both glasses of juice. Then I turn on cartoons for her. Once she's organized, I draw or paint with watercolours or maybe do a craft so mom can sleep in.

We try to stay quiet. She says us being able to entertain ourselves so she can sleep late is her weekend treat.

But this Saturday, she's up almost as early as we are and she's smiling, which is different. Our mom is not a morning person. That means she takes a long time to wake up and become herself and needs two cups of coffee before she wants to do anything.

"Come on, girls," she says, being all sparkly. "Go get dressed! Lots to do today!"

I'm wondering if this means driving around to all the

yard sales and garage sales. Could be, because they start early. I'm sure it's not a bunch of chores like cleaning the whole house, because doing that all day always makes her as cranky as it makes me feel.

But no. It's a garage sale day.

Mom doesn't just like garage sales. She *adores* garage sales. She goes kind of crazy at garage sales, buying lots of stuff and filling up the car. Then we unload it all in our garage and fix it up. It's kind of fun, especially when it's just mom and me.

Trying to keep track of Daisy at yard sales is less fun. She always wants to buy more toys and games and princess dresses and books, just like all the ones she's already got spread all over our room.

But today, it IS just mom and me.

Daisy and I hurry up and get dressed, and soon we're on our way to drop my sister off at Aunt Sorcha's house. Like just about everybody, she thinks Daisy is a sweetheart. She and Uncle Chris have two little boys that are twins. They're 3 years old. Daisy loves going over there to play with them.

She pretends to be their big sister.

Then mom and I are on to today's surprise, which turns out not to be going to garage sales, or at least not yet. Instead, we're going into Brighton, the next town up the coast from our town, because they have a Saturday Farmer's Market.

It's called Farmer's, because you can get vegetables and fruit and meat and even fish there. There are tables and chairs at one end, where you can sit and eat a sausage sandwich, or have a bowl of chowder or hot cider and a piece of pie. But there's also booths where you can buy jewellery, candles, soap, body lotions, sweaters and other things people make, like a craft fair.

Every time we go, there's something different to see, like furniture made out of driftwood, or birdfeeders made out of recycled bottles and cans, or hand-made chocolates shaped like clams and crabs and starfish, or the most interesting to me, the booth with watercolour paintings of fishing villages and the ocean by an artist whose work I really like. Her name is Maudie Adams.

Sometimes there are people playing fiddle music, but that's mostly in summer for the tourists.

"Are we here for lunch?" I ask my mom.

"We're here for lunch AND research," she says. She says research is finding out things you didn't already know that are true. The research is finding proof that they're true.

Our research turns out to be going to all the booths that have any kind of baked goods, likes pies, cakes, squares and cookies.

"We're taking a look at what they're selling," Mom says before taking some money from her purse and handing it to a bored-looking teenager. She hands mom a little tray with six teensie cookies that aren't much bigger than quarters. "It was your Aunt Sorcha's idea!" The girl puts the cookie tray in mom's forever shopping bag and hands her some coins.

Mom says thanks and we move on. She's smiling.

This doesn't happen often lately, so I think something must be up. After all, mom can make all the cookies she'd ever want, or a whole Saturday market full of people would want, so why are we here *buying* cookies?

And date bars.

And cake.

Is this because we're going to have a party? But why? It's isn't my birthday for two months, almost. Daisy already had her birthday. It won't be mom's birthday till next January. And Danny's is at Christmas-time.

I'm getting more and more curious, but I wait to ask till we're headed back to the car, both of us carrying a couple of bags of fresh veg, fruit and, of course, all those cookies.

"So, what's this research about?" I ask while mom is clicking her car remote so it will beep to remind her where we left the car.

"Well, partly eating them, but also seeing how much they cost," she says.

I really don't get it. Eating them? We already eat cakes and bars and cookies. A LOT. And seeing how much they cost? More than just making them at home, probably. "But, why?"

Instead of saying, "Oh, really, Morley, stop pestering me about this!" or "For goodness sake, Morley, wait and you'll see!" like she is always saying to me, she's still smiling, like she has a wonderful secret.

This is seriously strange.

She's smiling so much, it's like we've stepped back in time to last year, before Danny's whole job losing thing happened. I wonder if that's it. If Danny's coming back today, or maybe this week. And we're having a party. Because he's home again.

She's actually grinning. It makes her look prettier. And younger. I wish she could always be this way.

"Because we're going into the cookie business, Morley. You and me. Daisy, too, if she wants to help."

I'm so stunned I almost don't know what to say. No, I almost don't know what to think, which hardly ever happens.

"The COOKIE business?" I finally sputter. "But you have a job at school...?"

"Yes I do, and I intend to keep it. But we can also do the cookie business. At the market. Every Saturday morning." Mom says, looking over at me and laughing. If I've got a dumb look on my face and she's laughing at me, I really don't care. It's a long time since I've heard her laugh like this. About anything.

"You know my friend Doris...you know, at my book club..."

I nod.

"Well, she heard they have some spaces coming up at the market."

"Spaces? What does that mean?"

"People who sell things there, they rent their space.

That means they pay money to have the place to sell what they make. I'm getting one of spaces, starting next week."

I must have a surprised look on my face, because mom keeps talking, like she's trying to talk me into this crazy idea. But the truth is, I don't care how crazy it is, if it makes her this happy.

"You can come and help me sell, and..." she starts counting things off on her fingers and I'm glad she isn't driving anywhere yet. "We'll need to round up a table and a couple of chairs. And a tablecloth. And I'll need to get some plates to put the cookies on...and we'll need plastic wrap...bags and change..."

"Change?"

"You know, like dimes and quarters and paper money."

Oh yeah, I think. Most of the people selling stuff can only take cash. Mrs. Green calls cash "real money."

We did a unit on it last month. About how if you buy, say, a used video game for $15.95 and you give the store person $20, that means a $20 bill which is paper money, then they have to give you back your change. Figuring out how much change you get back is a math problem: $20 minus $15.95. The answer is $4.05, which means you would get back four dollars and five cents.

"You can help me with the selling and making change," Mom says. "It will be good practice for you and maybe help with your math grades."

I groan.

When I'm a grown-up and finished with school, the one thing I never ever want to do again is any math problems. Mom says that's being ridiculous, because everybody needs to be good at math. You have to use it every day of your life, she says. So, I might as well learn now.

She says learning is easier when you're still a kid.

She says I should be grateful I have the chance to go to school and learn things to make my life easier when I'm a grown-up.

She says a lot of kids don't have that chance. Millions of kids, around the world.

But I've stopped listening, because I'm still trying to think about this crazy cookie idea.

So now we're heading home, but mom can't resist stopping at some yard sales.

At the first one I find a floppy hat, kind of like my rain hat that I lost. It looks pretty clean, so I put it on and check out how I look in an old stand-up mirror.

"Why would you want that old thing?" Mom says, but she laughs when she says it. "Doesn't look much like a sunhat!"

I don't care because I like it. It feels good on and I wonder if wearing it would also be lucky, like my wish bracelets. So I get it, for three quarters. That's 75 cents.

Mom spots two beaten-up-looking folding chairs with faded pink fabric, the kind you might get for the beach. She buys them for $1 each with a $5 bill ($3 change).

"It's an omen, Morley!" she says happily. "We've got our market chairs. A sign our luck is changing!"

At the next place, she buys some old picture frames for us to fix up to frame more of my drawings. And she buys some cookie sheets and baking tools. I buy a box of beading stuff with some pretty glass beads and wire. The lady selling it says her daughter was into beading, but that was last year. Now, it's knitting. She's happy to see another young girl getting the jewellery-making supplies.

Me, too.

I find a party princess craft kit that Daisy might like, so I buy it for 50 cents. It looks like it's never even been opened! It's amazing what people pay good money for but never use, Mom says. "But good for us, because then we can have it!" she adds, in her happy voice.

We get home and unload everything and then, all afternoon long, we're tasting the bought cookies while I make bracelets.

Some of them are wish bracelets, in all the colours people have asked for. But I also try some fancier ones, using the directions in the friendship bracelet kit Sam gave me. Plus all the new beads and cord and jewellery wire in the box I got at the garage sale.

It's fun to try out different ideas and just play with the beads and think up new designs. Even though they're harder to make and take longer.

"That was a lucky find. And a lucky day for us!" Mom

says, handing me another cookie to taste. I'm going to be so stuffed I won't even want any dinner!

Those cookies we bought at the market are pretty good. But not nearly as good as mom's.

She's all excited like she hasn't been about anything since, well, I don't remember when.

She's looking at her recipes...

...and making lists of stuff she needs more of like flour and un-salted butter and eggs and raisins and spices...

...and talking about the prices of those cookies we bought, like this: "Imagine, Morley! The nerve of them, charging that much for such tiny little cookies there's only two bites to them!"

And thinking about where she's going to get a table we can fit in our car.

But that turns out to be another lucky omen, because the people who don't want their market space any more leave their two tables behind. And we already have those beat-up beach chairs, out in the garage. Mom cleans them up and I help paint them, ready to use on our first day at the market.

I have to admit it's fun helping mom start the cookie business. We call it mom's Yummy Cookies. That's my idea. I love how excited she is about it.

Mom says cookies are the best plan we've had in a long time.

It reminds me of my own plan, and I smile.

nine

That week, we bake mountains of cookies.

Daisy roars around, acting as crazy as ever.

The renters seem to be shouting and fighting all the time...

So it's pretty much an average week. Including...

...Julia the Jerk being nasty and calling me names like Fish Face and punching me some more when no one else is close enough to notice and I'm not quick enough to get away.

...Sam and Jayden being the best friends I could ever imagine having. All week they help me with the Get Morley's Pet project. And they help think up ways to get the Get Danny To Come Home project started.

...My wrist and ribs are healing at a speed that would make a turtle race look fast. But I'm starting to feel more like myself.

Or trying to.

Mom helps me push all the Daisy junk over to her side of our room and we paint a line down the middle. And arrange the furniture so we each have our own space.

Now, my side looks the way I want it to. Her side is still a mess, but it's easier to ignore it.

Daisy doesn't apologize, exactly, for what happened when she jumped out of the apple tree. She still thinks I should have caught her. But she does say sorry for your sore arm and sorry for your sore chest and I hear myself telling her that she's forgiven. She is so easy-going all the time, it's hard to stay mad at her. Even when I want to.

There's a bad moment when mom gets an e-mail from Danny. She reads parts of it to us:

Doing fine, though I've been moving around a lot. No address...

Like the new job...

Tell Morley to be a good girl and kiss my little sweetheart Daisy and tell her I'll visit soon and want her to...

Be good, I'm thinking. Aren't I always? And doesn't he even care that I got hurt?

"Oh," my mother says suddenly, her hand going to her mouth and sort of bending, as if she has a bad stomach pain. "Oh, no..."

Without another word, she goes to her bedroom and closes the door.

Daisy says she's hungry, so I get out bread and make her a peanut butter banana sandwich with the crusts cut off. I make myself a smoothie. We eat at the kitchen table, waiting for mom to come back.

Daisy wants to colour in her book that teaches letters and numbers and she wants me to help her. So I do. It's just easier to do what she wants than put up with her interrupting me all the time.

When Mum comes back to the kitchen, her face is red and puffy, like she's sick. Or she's been crying.

Daisy is watching *Toy Story* for like the ten-thousandth time and doesn't even notice.

I know better than to ask what's wrong and just keep trying to sketch, using my left hand to help my right hand. It's awkward, but at least I can draw again. Sort of.

"It's nothing, Morley..." Mom says at last. I can see that she's stirring more dough to make something.

I'd like to know more. But instead she asks about school (OK, I tell her), about Sam's party (going to be a surprise) and what I think I might get Sam for a gift (don't know yet), about Grandpa coming to visit soon, maybe for Thanksgiving, she says. Thanksgiving seems like a really long time away. It isn't even summer yet.

Mom talks and talks about everything except the things I really want to know.

Is Danny coming home? When? Why isn't he already here?

Or has he left because they're getting a divorce? This is the thing I'm worried about. I know about what divorce is, because Sam's parents are divorced. Her mom has a new boyfriend. Her dad has a new wife and they have three kids. Sam is an only child, but with half-brothers and a half-sister.

Sam has two bedrooms of her own, one at each of her homes. She has different clothes, different books and even different pets at each of her two homes.

I think this must get so confusing. Wouldn't you always be leaving the exact thing you want at the other house? And wouldn't you just be used to living at one place when you have to change to the other? But Sam says it's not so bad, once you get used to it.

I guess she didn't have a choice, but I wouldn't want that to happen to our family. Which is another reason I want Danny to come home.

That week mom – or mom and I – do lots of baking. She shows me more about how and lets me do more than she ever has before. She isn't happy, like she was at the farmer's market, but she isn't crabby, either.

I try to ask about Danny and where he is. And if he found his job there. But she just changes the subject.

After lots of looking at her recipes, she has decided to make just six different things to sell on our first market day. They're all going to be from the recipes she learned from her grandmother, she says, just like I'm learning now.

"People like good home cooking. Much better than

what you can buy in a box from the store," she says. I hope other people think so, too.

We make mint chocolate chip cookies with big chunks of chocolate. And maple syrup squares, apple carrot cake, sweet scones, chewie butterscotch brownies and my favourite, strawberry jam-jams.

We find little paper plates at the dollar store, the kind you have at parties. We buy all the ones in our favorite colors.

We arrange the cookies on the plates, covering each with plastic wrap and add a sticky label telling what kind of cookie it is and the price.

Friday evening, mom loads up the car with the two folding chairs, the sign I made to go in a little standing picture frame that tells what types of cookies and bars we've got and what they cost and then all the wrapped little plates. There's 60 of them, 10 of each kind.

"Everything's going to be $4," Mom explains. "So, making change is going to be really simple!"

The market doesn't open until 8 a.m. Long before that, we're up, mom's had coffee, the car is packed up and we're on the way to drop off Daisy for a play-date at her friend Rachel's house.

Then it's on to the market. We're directed to a place almost at the middle of the main market building, which looks like a really big barn, except it's clean and made out of cement, not barnwood.

When we find our space, there's a beat-up kitchen table and a picnic table and nothing else.

"This is great," Mom says, covering the tables with two pretty table cloths she found at a garage sale. We set up the chairs, arrange the plates of cookies, put up the sign and mom hands me an apron with pockets like hers. She also has an old fishing tackle box that must have come from a yard sale, but I don't remember ever seeing it before. That's for our money, mom says. "Just like the bank, when we're playing Monopoly. Only with real money!" she says, grinning like it's a great joke.

There's still 15 minutes until the doors open for customers. "Remember what I told you," Mom says.

I do remember. Smile at people. Tell them it's fun to make these cookies, the same kinds Gran makes. This isn't true, because our Gran died a long time ago. Before I was born. But we are using her recipes, so mom says that's OK.

If they buy something, count out their change carefully, so you are sure it's right.

Be sure to always say, "Thank you."

Mom goes off to get another coffee and a juice drink for me. I sit there, looking around, wondering what else to do. Our booth might be almost the smallest one there, but I think it looks nice. The scones, cookies and bars all look yummy. We've cut up some and put them on a plate for people to try free samples.

There are butterflies in my stomach, but mom says this is going to work. "We can do this, Morley," she says. I want to believe her. I look up and the teenage girl at the next booth smiles at me and I think she's not that much older than me, maybe 13 or 14.

Suddenly mom is back and people are starting to come in and someone is asking mom if she uses real chocolate in her brownies and someone else takes two packages of squares and hands me a $10 bill. I say thank you and give him his change ($2) and he walks away, not saying one single word.

But it doesn't matter because there's a woman right behind him who wants to know if we're sure there are absolutely no peanuts in these cookies? How do I know there aren't? I tell her it's because I helped make them. She just sniffs and walks away, but mom says never mind, some people are just funny.

A lady asks if we sell bracelets like the ones I'm wearing on my left arm. I'm not sure what to say, but mom says, "Not with us today, but we're happy to take your order and deliver, if you live in town? Or we'll be here next Saturday, if you want to get them then?"

The lady describes what she wants and it sounds really easy – four wish bracelets in gold, green, orange and royal blue. I tell her they'll be $2 each. mom writes down the order and the lady's name and phone number.

Then we get super busy. It seems like everyone in our town is here at the market. All the chocolate mint chip cookies are sold, and most of the brownies and a lot of everything else when things kind of slow down.

"Can you hold the fort for 10 minutes?" Mom wants to know.

I say ok. Mom refills the free samples plate and goes to offer a taste to the neighbour vendors. I hear her saying that she's Eefa, from over in Seabright, and nice to meet you. She asks what their favourite kind of cookie is. I wonder if this is more cookie research. Or maybe she's just making friends.

She comes back with hot dogs and drinks and we eat at our booth, in between talking to people.

We're just about finished eating when a man comes up to our tables. "Eefa!" he says, as if he's knows my mum and he's surprised to see her.

She smiles. "Morley," she says, "This is our new principal, Mr. Maclean." I remember that the principal is my mom's boss. He puts out his hand, as if to take some cookies, just when I'm offering him a free sample, holding the plate with my left hand.

Mr. Maclean's hand and the sample plate collide and the little pieces of cookie spill all over the place.

Everything freezes. I can feel my face getting hot.

"Er, so sorry," Mr. Maclean says, exactly when mom is saying, "Not a problem, really."

And I'm trying to pick up all the little pieces and put them back on the plate, feeling my face flaming hot.

"Here, let me pay for ..." Mr. Maclean says.

"Don't even think of it," Mom says, as if she's not the least bit bothered.

But he insists, so in the end Mr. Maclean hands me $12 and takes three plates of scones (no change) and I do the smile-thank-you like I've been told to, remembering to look our customer right in the eyes. That's when I notice he has nice eyes. They're very deep brown and they look like they're interested in what you're saying.

I can tell my mom likes him.

"Good to meet you, Morley – and good luck with your new venture, Eefa. See you Monday!" he says, moving off.

"He's nice," I say to mom, noticing her watching him walk away.

"Most people are," is all she says.

At noon, Caitlin, who is the market manager, comes around to collect our booth rent. Mom takes three $10 bills and a $5 bill (total, $35) from our fishing tackle cash box, hands them to Caitlin and asks for a receipt. Caitlin says she'll email it and she hopes she'll be seeing us next week. Mom says, "Absolutely!"

Then it's 1 p.m., closing time. I can't believe it's been five hours that we've been here, the time went by so quickly. We have only four plates of cookies left. Mom trades them to other vendors for a bag of tomatoes and a cyclamen plant that is just about to bloom.

It takes almost no time for us to pack up. Mom counts up the money in the cash box while I fold the tablecloths, the picture frame sign and our two chairs, ready to carry back to the car.

"Congratulations, Morley! We made some money today, and it was fun, wasn't it? I'm really pleased at how this worked. Are you?"

I wonder if this might be a good time to talk about getting a pet and why I want one so badly.

Or ask about what Danny meant about visiting soon. And I want to write to him, but I don't know his address.

Or what else he said in his e-mail that she didn't tell us, but it makes her so upset.

But she's still going on about the market and everyone she met...

...and what sold really well so we should make more for next time...

...and what she'd like to do differently. Maybe the prices weren't right? Or she should have done some cakes? Or put up a sign saying she could take orders for different kinds of cookies?

I just say "Um, yeah," and "Uh-huh" and she keeps talking.

She tells me about the woman who owns a café over in Porter's Bay who wants someone to make cakes for her, if mom is interested, which she is...

And someone else asked about if we offer cupcakes, and mom said yes, we sure do, so they ordered two dozen (this means 24) for next market day, for a birthday party...

And how nice that vendor woman was who she traded with to get the tomatoes...

...and I decide that, for once, it's better if I just *listen*.

Is she happy and excited, more than just about any

time I can remember? Yes.

Am I pleased? Mostly, yes. It was fun. I liked seeing how my mom answered questions, and how she talked about what we baked together; how proud she was of our cookies.

I liked talking to the people who wanted to buy something. It was even kind of fun to figure out how to make change.

When she says she's proud of me, and how much help I was, it feels like the best day ever, for as long as I can remember. I'm good at what she calls "being organized and dealing with people."

So, how would I feel about getting $25 for all my good work with the baking and helping today? And the same every week, for doing the cookies business?

I'm pretty excited to say yes! That's another $25 every week to add to my savings to get a pet. Mom is always saying how having a pet costs money, so I figure if I help pay for my pet, then maybe, just maybe, she'll finally say, "yes!"

Do I want to do the cookie business again next week? "Sure," I say. "Why not?"

"Because we make a great team, Morley, you and me," Mom says, hugging me, being careful to be gentle.

But I'm also really tired. This kind of tired makes my wrist and chest start to ache again.

Once we get home, I think about sketching but end up on the couch with the remote and a root beer float for a treat.

Soft, the kitten upstairs says in my head. *Warm.
Sleepy.*

I feel the same way, I tell him, wondering if he hears
me.

ten

Get up when mom calls us, make Daisy get up, pull on my school uniform, help Daisy into her pink princess dress because she insists on wearing it every single day, eat cereal, grab my bag lunch from the fridge and stuff it in my backpack, brush my teeth, make Daisy brush her teeth and get out to the car before Mum yells at us.

That's pretty much what happens every morning. Except for the mornings that I have to get the garbage bin from the end of our driveway and drag it back to the side of our house.

It's a garbage bin morning when Daisy decides she doesn't want to go to school. It's a beautiful day, the first warm day of spring. Daisy she wants us to go to the beach.

Mom is explaining this isn't going to happen, and why can't Daisy just be reasonable? Daisy is waving her arms around and has a face that looks like a thundercloud. That always means she's just about to go into a major Daisy meltdown.

I grab my backpack, toss it next to the car and go out to the street for the garbage bin. While I'm dragging it back towards where it always sits next to the garage, for some reason I look up at the balcony on our house. Mom is just pulling Daisy out the front door and locking it.

And that's when I see it and why my mother and sister don't.

Our house has a balcony at the front. It has a door from the upstairs living room. This balcony is also the roof over the front door and front porch, and that's next to our driveway. When you're at the front door, you might hear people up on the balcony, but you can't see them.

Scared, the upstairs kitten says in my head. *Loud. Scared. Hurt. Hide!*

Mom, still wrangling herself, her tote bag, Daisy's backpack and a screeching Daisy out the front door and locking it, can't see what's going on up on the balcony. But I'm standing on the sidewalk, so I have a clear view.

I could close my eyes right now and still see it.

The upstairs renter woman is outside, holding onto their baby and also what looks like a stuffed toy. The man is right next to her, shouting something. It sounds like swearing. He's shouting really loud, but I don't understand what he's saying. I think it isn't English. Or at least, not in any words I've ever heard.

But you can tell he's furious about something. The woman is backing away, as if she thinks he's going to hit her.

Then, suddenly, the man grabs the baby's toy by a leg and swings it around above his head.

Pain, pain, PAIN, the kitten screams in my head.

And then the man throws it.

And whatever it is, it's coming straight at me, like a frozen black and white snowball. Or maybe a softball. It's about that big.

*Falling...falling...falling...*the kitten screams.

I might have screamed myself as I jumped out of the way, afraid that the toy, or whatever it is, is going to hit me.

And then, with a THUNK, it lands right in front of me, on the grass right next to the driveway.

I look up to see the man, still yelling, grabbing the woman's hair. As she shrieks and their baby starts to howl, he drags her back inside and slams the balcony door.

By now my mother is struggling to buckle Daisy into her car seat, while Daisy is kicking and skreeching about how she doesn't want to go to school, she wants Danny to take her to the beach.

"Morley," Mom shouts over all this Daisy noise. "Come on! Leave the bin for now! We're already late!"

But, on the other side of the garbage bin, so my mom can't really see, I've gotten closer to get a look at what it was the upstairs man threw off the balcony. If it was their baby's toy, I probably should return it. Or at least give it to mom to give back.

But it isn't a toy. Or any of the other things I thought it might be when it was falling towards me.

It's hardly bigger than my hand. A tight little ball, so soft it's like touching feathers. It's breathing.

"Feather..." I whisper.

Pain. Pain. Pain.

"Morley," Mom yells. "Stop fooling around and get in the car. NOW!"

"But it's a kitten. Mom, wait, please, it's a kitten and it's hurt bad!"

"Just LEAVE it Morley! It's probably a stray. Its mother will find it..."

"But it's hurt!" I shout over all the Daisy noise.

The kitten is curled up in a ball, with its eyes closed. There is blood around its mouth.

Then, for no reason at all, what Danny said came into my mind.

"Tell Morley to be a good girl." That's what he said. That's what he wanted me to know.

Be good.

It was a message. And now I know what it means.

Because isn't helping others being good? Especially when they are smaller than you and weaker than you and they're hurt?

"For God's sake, it's probably just lost, so just leave it be, Morley! And GET IN THIS CAR NOW!"

There's no time to stop and think.

With my back to the car, I scoop up the kitten, tuck him inside my jacket and get in the back seat. Mom is still telling Daisy to "just calm down" and promising that we'll go to the beach soon. Maybe after school today. She doesn't even notice me.

Telling Daisy to be quiet never works, so instead I whisper to her that I have a special secret, but I wouldn't tell her until she stops bawling.

Pain, the kitten says. *Pain.*

You're safe, I tell him, in my mind. *I'll help you.*

By the time I get my seatbelt done up, Daisy has mostly stopped carrying on and mom, with her serious face on but not saying anything, is clicking on the car radio.

"The surprise is a story," I whisper to Daisy. "It's about a fairy princess called Daisy who lives in a magic fairyland made of pink cake with candy clouds…"

Mom doesn't say anything, she just drives. I wonder if she's listening. She's probably just thinking about something else.

But at least the car is quiet, except for me telling the story and the Taylor Swift music mom has playing.

Of course, the fairy story isn't finished by the time we get to school, but that was my plan. "No more crying," I whisper to Daisy, "no shrieking and no kicking the back of the seat and if you're the happy Daisy ALL DAY I'll tell you the rest of the story at bedtime."

Daisy bounces out of the car and up to the door being all smiley and chatty, as if nothing has happened. While mom is saying hello to her kindergarten teacher and getting Daisy in the door, I lift Feather out of the place under my jacket where he'd been snuggled.

There is a whimper from him as I move him into my backpack.

I know he's hurt. I know it's now my responsibility to get help for him. Somehow. As mom drives around to the back of the school and parks and says things about me hurrying up and see you later and have a good day – the stuff she always says – my brain is thinking and thinking about how I'm going to save Feather.

And then maybe, when he's better, he'll be my kitten.

Because those upstairs people don't want him. They threw him away.

Like he was just a piece of garbage.

Not anything they wanted.

But I want him.

He called out to me.

He was falling.

He was frightened.

I could have caught him.

But I didn't.

I didn't leap forward and catch him. He fell to the ground and now, he's hurt bad.

And I know exactly what *that* feels like.

eleven

The morning announcements are just starting when I slide into my seat. Mrs. Green is writing on the blackboard, so she doesn't notice that I'm almost late.

As mom would say, on this morning there are more important things to worry about than being a minute or two late.

Any time I can, I sneak a look at Feather. He's curled up in my backpack. It's hung up on my hook, on the wall next to our classroom's door. My group table is on the other side of the room, over near the windows, about as far away from him as I could be.

I worry.

Each time I look, he's not exactly sleeping, but not awake, either. He doesn't open his eyes.

He doesn't say much except *pain...pain...pain...*

His voice is getting softer.

Weaker.

We have silent reading, then we have natural environments and talk about whales, then there is something about the times tables, but I'm having a hard time paying attention.

The whole time I'm thinking, how can I help Feather? He's hurt, and I don't know what to do.

But then I think – Jayden will know. He has pets and his family lives on a farm, with lots of animals. AND his mom is a doctor for animals.

The morning drags on. We go outside for gym class and play on the tennis court. We don't have any real tennis rackets, though, just some old broken badminton ones.

Finally, it's recess. I grab my backpack and race outside, looking everywhere for Jayden.

I spot him playing kick-ball with some other kids. I don't want to leave my backpack on the ground, so I just watch.

Recess is almost over when Jayden and Sam finally come over to where I'm sitting.

As quickly as I can, I tell them about the upstairs people, the man who threw Feather off the balcony and about him being in my backpack. Then I show them.

"Wow!" Sam says. "What are you going to do?"

I don't know.

"Maybe it's a barn cat," Jayden says. "They're usually pretty good at looking after themselves. Or a feral cat. You know, a cat that's wild."

"No," I say, "I don't think so. The upstairs people have a little kid. Feather has to be a pet. And he's still really little. Just a kitten."

"OK," Jayden says. "I'll call Mom at lunch time. I think this is her day at the pet shelter. She'll know what to do."

"But going to a vet costs money..." I say, just as the bell rings.

"Don't worry," Sam says, as we walk back towards our classroom. "I'll help you. And I know Jayden will, too."

Then Mrs. Green is telling us we're going to do a writing assignment. We need to write a story about something real that happened in our life last week. Or in the last few days. That means it's true and it happened not long ago.

It can't be something we did in a video game or saw on TV. "Something in your real life," she says.

"Morley," she says, and I jump. Am I in trouble? Does she suspect something? "You can sit with me at the back and tell me your story and I'll write it down. OK, everyone, you have five minutes to plan your story and 20 minutes to write it."

Then she walks to the back of our class and points to the two chairs in the free reading area. She sits down with a pad of paper, clicks her pen and says, "OK, Morley, what's your story going to be?"

I try to think. Something real that happened recently.

I could tell about selling cookies and wish bracelets at the market.

Or about what it's like to have a broken wrist and a cast on it.

Or about Daisy jumping out of the treehouse.

But all I can think of right now is Feather.

Feather falling.

Me picking him up and tucking him in my jacket. Next to my heart.

So that's the story I tell her.

Mrs. Green doesn't say anything. She's writing and frowning. I get to the end.

"And where is this kitten now?" she says.

I tell her.

"I see," she says. "Go back to your seat now, Morley. We'll talk about this at lunch time."

She goes back to the front of the room and tells everyone they should be finishing up by now and to put their names on the top of their paper and hand them forward.

Then Mrs. Green is talking again, something about the explorers and 1654, when the first settlers arrived from France to start our town, Seabright. But all I can think about is Feather.

And about the No Pets rule at our house. But the renters had a pet, didn't they? They had Feather.

Now I have him. When I get home, I'll tell mom I'm going over to Jayden's house. His mom will be there, after she comes home from work. I'll ask her to look after Feather. I'll give her my birthday and Christmas money. And the money I'm making from selling the wish bracelets at the market and at school. Lots of kids saw the ones I made for Jayden and Sam. I already have to make about 20 bracelets I've promised people.

I hope Jayden's mum can help save Feather.

I hope my mum understands.

I hope this school day ends soon, because I've got more important things to do than sit here while Mrs. Green drones on and on about people from Europe saying they were discovering North America, when there were already people living here, like they had been for thousands and thousands of years.

Stupid explorers!

twelve

We only get 20 minutes for lunch, so I was hurrying to meet up with Jayden and Sam when Mrs. Green said, "Morley. Stay behind, please."

Some of the other kids snickered. "Oh, oh, Sorely Poorly Morley's in trouble again!" I heard Tiffany say.

"Get your things and follow me!" Mrs. Green says, marching through the door and along the hall. I don't need to ask where we're going.

"Sit there!" She points at one of the hard chairs, when we get to the office.

That's where my mother works. Her desk is behind the counter and just outside the Principal's Office. It used to be mean old Lumpy Lumley, but he's gone and we have this new principal. Mr. Maclean.

He seemed nice when I met him at the Saturday market. He bought some cookies and the next week he bought one of my bracelets. But maybe he wouldn't be nearly as nice once Mrs. Green tells him I brought a pet to school today. Without permission.

Whatever that was, it isn't going to be half as bad as what my mother says when she finds out.

But luckily, my mother isn't at her desk.

I check on Feather.

He's breathing fast.

His eyes are closed.

It looks like the bleeding has stopped.

Feather makes a little kitten sound, like a mew.

I know he's too hurt for me to hold him.

I stroke his head, very gently.

I wait.

The red second hand on the big clock on the office wall moves, click-click-click-click.

Four minutes pass.

Five.

Eight.

It's quiet. No one else comes into the office.

The phone rings. It stops after three rings.

I wonder where my mother has gone. Out to lunch, maybe. Or to do errands. I hope she doesn't walk back in any minute now and find me here. Waiting to see the principal.

I wonder what Jayden and Sam think, since I didn't turn up to have lunch with them.

I wonder about where Danny is right now. If he misses us. If he'd help me get Feather looked after.

If he was here.

I wonder about how hurt Feather is. He fell on the grass. Not on the sidewalk or the driveway. I hope that makes a difference. Makes him less hurt.

If I'd caught him, maybe he wouldn't be hurt at all.

I wonder about how good kittens are at getting better, after they get hurt because they fall off a balcony.

Or get thrown off.

If maybe they're better at getting better after falling than kids are.

Or if all hurt animals get better quicker than people do.

If it hurts just as much. I think it probably does.

And I wonder how long Mrs. Green and Mr. Maclean are going to talk. I wish I could hear what they're saying. About Feather and what happened to him.

About me. And what I did.

But all I can hear is a sort of grumble-rustle-rustle-grumble. It sounds like when you have a movie on, but the sound turned way down. So you just about *almost* hear it.

But not really.

So you just wonder. Or worry.

Suddenly, the door bursts open and Mrs. Green, looking really mad about something, stomps out. She doesn't look at me.

"Come on in, Morley," Mr. Maclean says pleasantly, "and have a seat." There's a dish of sour gummies on his desk. I don't want any.

I wonder if he's going to start yelling. Like old Lumpy Lumley always did.

But Mr. Maclean is using his inside voice. "I like those cookies I got at your booth at the market," he said. "You and your mum made them, right? Thank you."

I don't know what to say, so I just wait.

He's still smiling. I'm wondering when he'll get to the angry part about having a cat in class. I hope he doesn't shout.

"And it looks like you're getting better. Everyone here at school is happy to see that you're just about back to being yourself."

"Um...yes," I say. Maybe not quite everyone. Like Julia and her bully gang of mean girls. "Yeah. I'm OK. Pretty much."

"We're happy to have you back with us, Morley. And I know your mother is very relieved that you're so much better..."

I don't say anything.

"She went home this morning. Bit of a tummy bug, she said. Nothing to worry about. I promised to tell you that she expects you to walk home from school today. Or take the bus."

"OK," I say.

"But we need to talk about something else, don't we?"

I look down at my shoes. Feather is sleeping now, but I know he's getting weaker. I can feel it.

"Morley," he says. "I know you found a kitten today and tried to rescue it. Can I see?"

I open my backpack and Mr. Maclean bends over to get a look.

"He's so hurt," I say, "he's hurting now..."

"I know," Mr. Maclean says. "But we're going to help him"

"We...?"

"Yes, Morley. We. You and me. And Mrs. Green already helped, by telling me what's going on.

"This is a big problem. Too big for a child to fix by herself, Morley. Even a brave and kind girl like you. An animal that's seriously hurt is a grown-up problem. So let me help you. Can I do that? Will you trust me to help you and this poor little kitten?"

He stops talking and looks at me, waiting for my answer.

Can I trust him?

Mr. Maclean is looking like he really wants to know what I have to say. He doesn't look mad and ready to yell at me, like you expect a principal to be. He looks kind. And like he really is worried about Feather.

So I say yes.

I don't know what else to do.

"Right," he says, pulling out his phone. "Just hold on while I make a couple of quick calls, and then we'll be on our way!"

He steps out of his office, leaving me sitting there. On our way to where, I wonder. To see the vet? And will it be Jayden's mum? I don't have my money with me. If we're going to the vet, how will I pay for Feather's care?

I reach in to touch his soft fur.

He's still breathing. That means he's still alive.

"You're going to get better," I whisper to him. "You'll be all right. I promise."

I really, really want my promise to come true.

I *need* it to come true.

Then Mr. Maclean is back, putting on his jacket, telling me to put on mine. We're going to get help for the kitten, he says. I wonder what he means, but there's no time to think about it. He picks up my backpack and we walk out to the parking lot and get in his car.

He says to do up the seatbelt.

He tells me we're going to Sunflower Pet Rescue Shelter. It's not far, he says.

I already know a little bit about it because Jayden says that's where his mum is the vet one afternoon every week. And that's where Sam got Tippy.

On the way to the pet shelter, Mr. Maclean asks about how I found the kitten, and why I brought him to school.

I tell him the same story I told Mrs. Green. And also about the No Pets Rule at our house.

Mr. Maclean doesn't act like I'm just a kid and I don't know things. He doesn't interrupt.

The pet shelter isn't very big. It's in what used to be a store. There are some chairs and a counter at the front. It looks a bit like the office at school, except that there are posters on the walls with pictures of dogs and cats.

"Hi there," the woman behind the counter says. She looks super young, like a teenager. But she must be a grown-up, or else she'd be in school. She's doing something on a computer, but stops when we come in. "Are you the ones that just called?"

Mr. Maclean says we are.

There are dogs barking somewhere. A woman with a clipboard comes out from the back, but she doesn't look at us. She just reaches inside my backpack and lifts out Feather. Then she turns around and walks through the door at the back. I follow her.

She walks so fast I can hardly keep up. We go past three doors, then she pushes a door open at the very end of the hall and tries to shut it before I get there.

"You're not allowed back here," she says. "You'll need to wait out front."

"But I need to know…." I say.

She slips through the door and I hear it make that *click* doors make when you lock them. So, I go back to the front to see Mr. Maclean reading a paper with a lot of writing on it. The front desk woman is doing something on her computer.

Smells. Dog. Bad. Fear. Pain. PAIN. PAIN. Hide! Feather says in my head.

Bad place. Bad place. Dog. Fear.

"You'll help him?" I ask the woman. "You'll help him get better?"

"That's what we do here," she says. "We help pets find good homes."

"His name is Feather," I say. "Lucky Feather."

"All the animals here are lucky," the woman says. "We give them good care until they find their forever homes."

"But he's hurt bad. He needs the vet. Doctor Van Haan." Jayden's mom.

"The kitten is with the vet now. It might be Dr. Van Haan. I don't know. But thank you for bringing him to us. You're a very responsible girl."

"Lucky Feather," I say. "His name is Lucky Feather."

"Um...yes. Well, like I said, all our cats and dogs are lucky to be here. They're getting a second chance for a home and a loving family. The kit...err, Feather... will get the very best care. If it's possible to save him, we will."

"If...?

"If we can save him," she says. "All we can do is try."

"But when...?" I ask. "How will I know he's better and

ready to go home?" With me, I'm thinking. When can Feather come home with me? How will I get my mother to say he can?

"Will you call me when he's ready to come home? And how much will it cost? I have money. I can pay..." I don't know how I'll pay for Feather's care, but I'll figure out something. I have to! Maybe my birthday and Christmas money that I've saved up, plus my money from selling cookies and bracelets will be enough.·

I hope so.

Mr. Maclean takes out a pen and signs a paper. The woman takes it. "And your little girl understands...?" she says. "That you're surrendering the kitten to us and that, given what you've told me, there may be an investigation?"

I don't know what this means. But it doesn't sound right.

Feather is still so frightened and he's hurting so much it is causing a pain in my head and in my stomach. But then, suddenly, he's asleep and breathing a bit better.

And then it feels like maybe I can breathe, too.

A second chance, the woman said. A second chance.

For a family.

For our family.

"I know you want the kitten to get better. And you wish he could be yours," Mr. Maclean says when we get back to his car. "But you know, Morley, he's very badly hurt. He might not be strong enough to live. And he isn't your cat. He belongs to someone else."

I don't want any of this to be true. But I know that it is.

"And I talked to your mother. She says she knows you want a pet, but it doesn't work for your family to have one right now."

I sit in the car and stare at my hands. I don't say anything.

"I'm so sorry, Morley. But you did the right thing. You used your head and your heart. You got help for that poor little kitten. That's what matters. He needed help and you helped him and because of that, now he is getting the medical care he needs.

"He's very lucky to have a friend like you."

"Feather," I say. "Lucky Feather. He's asleep right now..."

"Yes. Like you were, after your accident."

I think about that. "But he'll wake up soon?"

"I don't know, Morley. I hope so. I know you hope so. That Feather is strong, that the vet and her assistants can save his life. That he'll grow up to be a normal, healthy cat. I hope that happens. But we know he's very hurt."

I do know that. And I know exactly what it feels like when you fall. And you can't breathe. And your body's broken.

And it hurts. Bad.

"When he gets better, can we adopt Lucky Feather at school? I mean, for a classroom pet?" Maybe Mrs. Green won't like this, but Jayden's teacher, Mr. Cadeau, is a cool guy. He might.

Mr. Maclean looks sad and I know he's going to tell me there's a rule about that. "Classroom pets need to be creatures that live in a tank or a cage, like a bearded dragon or a gerbil. That's because we can't have animals wandering around the room, disturbing students who are there to learn. It would be too distracting."

I understand. Who wouldn't rather play with a kitten than sit and do their school work?

Then I notice that Mr. Maclean has turned onto Main Street towards our house, instead of taking the way back to school.

Mr. Maclean says, "there isn't much left of the school day, Morley. So I'll just drop you off at home."

I can just imagine what my mother is going to say. That THE PRINCIPAL had to bring me home. I wonder if I can get into the house without her noticing.

But Mr. Maclean parks his car behind ours and we walk to the front door.

It opens, but not with my mother standing there. It's Aunt Eira. She smiles at Mr. Maclean.

"Oh, Morley, good," she says. "And you are...?"

Mr. Maclean introduces himself.

Aunt Eira invites him in for coffee.

He says he has to get back. But perhaps another time.

These are the kinds of things adults say to each other, instead of talking about important things.

I duck around my aunt and head for my room. Our room.

But a moment later, my aunt is there, knocking gently on the door. She probably isn't going to go away and leave me alone, so I let her in.

"You look like you've had a rough day," she says.

That's the last thing I expected. I can't help it. I start to cry.

I cry and cry and cry until all the water in me is used up. Aunt Eira holds me and rocks me as if I'm a really little kid and I fell and scraped my knee.

I wish I had, because this hurts so much more.

I know what surrender means. It means give up. I gave up having Feather. I gave him away to the pet shelter. Or Mr. Maclean did.

But I let it happen.

So Feather would get better.

He could have internal injuries, the woman at the shelter said. That means inside his body. He might have a broken jaw. He's badly hurt.

I know this.

I want it not to have happened.

I want him to be well and happy, like any healthy kitten.

And I want him to be my kitten. In my family.

I try to hear him in my mind, but he's gone. Maybe he's too far away. Maybe he's still asleep, after an operation to fix whatever he has that was broken.

Maybe he was so hurt that the vet couldn't save him.

I don't know, but he's gone from my head. It makes me feel so alone.

All I can do is cry.

thirteen

It makes me boiling mad when people think kids are stupid, or dishonest, just because they aren't grown-ups yet. But that's exactly what Mrs. Green is doing.

What she's saying right now is everyone is free to go to recess.

Except me.

Other kids are quick to get out the door. Then I'm standing there, in front of her desk and she's writing something and frowning.

Making me just stand there and wait.

And then she's saying that sometimes children tell tales because they don't know the difference between what really happens and what just happens in their imagination.

"If I've learned anything in my 35 years of teaching, Morley, it's that children exaggerate," she says. "And they also lie. All the time."

It's as if she thinks adults never do this. But I know they do.

"And I know you're a very imaginative girl, Morley," she adds, in her stern voice. "With all the little doodles you make and the story-telling."

"You mean, with my art work. And writing."

"Well, if you want to call it that. But I'm more concerned about this story you told about a cat..."

"Feather," I said, not caring that I'm interrupting. "His name is Lucky Feather. He's a kit..."

"About this cat," she says, "that you say you saw falling off a balcony, so you brought it to school yesterday, which you know is not allowed. Our classroom is for learning. It's not a zoo."

This brings an idea into my mind of drawing a classroom where all the students are animals. Happy animals, so I smile.

"This is no laughing matter," She says.

I look at her, trying to remember if I've ever seen Mrs. Green laugh, ever. About anything. Or even smile.

"So, is that a true story you wrote yesterday? Or just a piece of fiction you made up to get attention?"

If I wanted to get attention, I can think of lots of ways of doing it, but I don't tell her this.

"It's non-fiction. That means something that really happened. What you told us we had to write yesterday. Something real that happened in our lives recently, and..."

I expect her to get angry about me being sassy, what she calls "talking back." Then I'll just duck out and get outside to recess. But instead, she says, "I see. Tell me this non-fiction of yours again, then."

I wish she'd just read the story I handed in, because I'd rather be outside, talking to Sam and Jayden and the other kids.

Mrs. Green says tell the story. So I do.

About Daisy taking too long to get ready, like every morning.

About hauling the garbage bin back towards the side of our house, while my mother and Daisy were still getting outside.

About the man yelling, and yanking the woman by the hair, and her shrieking, and him grabbing something and throwing it.

About it coming down and landing on the grass, right at my feet.

About looking closer to see it was a kitten.

About my mom yelling for me to hurry up and get in the car.

About scooping up the kitten and hiding him in the front of my jacket.

Then in my backpack.

"And where is this kitten now?" she says when I finish. "I hope it isn't still over there in your backpack?" she points towards the row of hooks on the wall.

"No," I say. He's at the..."

But the bell sounds then. Kids are coming back into the room.

Mrs. Green waves me towards my seat. "Thank you, Morley," she says. "I just needed a better understanding of your story." She turns to write something on the board.

Sam looks over with a questioning look on her face when she comes back in. I just shrug my shoulders and mouth, "Tell you at lunch."

"OK," she says, smiling. I know she was worried for me. She's always saying if you just act nice all the time to grown-ups and say what they want to hear, they'll mostly leave you alone.

I try to do that. But sometimes, I just get so mad, what I'm really thinking spills out.

Usually, I wish this didn't happen. Not because I get in trouble, but because they're my real thoughts. Other people don't deserve to know what I'm really thinking and feeling, especially other people like old sourpuss Mrs. Green.

My aunt Eira says when I get mad, I should just take a really deep breath and think for a minute before I say anything.

She says that there are always annoying people. You have to learn how to get along with them. Even when you don't want to.

And she says the thing to remember about Mrs. Green is that I'm going to pass Grade 5, but she isn't. She'll still be here, teaching another group of grade 5s next year.

If so, I feel sorry for them.

But then I cheer up, thinking that it isn't too long now till summer vacation. And only three more weeks till Sam's birthday party.

Maybe mom will take Daisy and me to visit Lucky Feather at the pet shelter today. Or tomorrow. After Saturday market, when she's in a good mood because we sold lots of her cookies. That's my plan.

Because I have to know that Feather is doing OK.

At lunchtime, I come out the school door looking around for Sam and Jayden. Then someone grabs me from behind, shoving me hard against the wall.

"Hey Duck-face!" Julia says, leaning against me as I try to push her away. "Wha-did-ja bring to school today? More animals? Or some of that stinky stuff your friend eats for lunch, what's it called, kim-PEE? Ha, ha!"

"It's kimchi, you dummy," I say, heaving Julia off me. My friend Sam is half Korean. Her mom came here from Korea to go to university and stayed when she married Sam's dad. Sam sometimes gets what Korean kids eat in her lunchbox, along with chopsticks, which I think is cool, even though Sam says she'd rather just have a sandwich.

I see Sam and Jayden coming towards us and call out to them. Julia turns away, as if she's going to go harass some other poor kid.

But then suddenly she grabs my wrist, the left one, not the right one that still has a cast on it. She yanks on one of my bracelets. It breaks, and yellow beads scatter on the ground.

"Ewww, boo hoo. Your stupid bracelet fell apart," Julia says. "Are you going to cry, crybaby?"

But I'm thrilled. Happier than I've been all day so far.

Because the bracelet she broke is the wish bracelet with the golden yellow beads. That's the one for my pet wish.

For Lucky Feather.

And that means I'm going to get him.

For our family. For me.

Really, really soon.

fourteen

My drawing of Jayden riding Spirit is finished. Mom says she thinks it's one of the best drawings I've ever done.

She helps me frame it and we wrap it up and take it over to his place.

We've put hooks and a wire on the back, so all Jayden has to do is decide where he wants to hang it up in his room.

We do that, while our moms sit in the kitchen and have tea and chat. Dr. Van Haan, Jayden's mom, says when she goes to the shelter, she'll check on the little kitten I helped rescue.

She says she'll let me know.

I say I'd be very grateful to hear about Lucky Feather.

Mom doesn't say anything.

Later, back at home, mom's baking again, in her old pajamas with the faded roses on them, sort of humming a tune to herself. This is a good sign. I think she's excited about the Saturday market. Or I hope so.

And Daisy is drawing fairies. Her drawing is pretty good, for a little kid.

It's an ordinary evening after dinner. We're all quiet and happy. Even the upstairs people are quiet. I can't say if they're happy because I haven't seen them since two days ago, when the renter man grabbed the woman and threw Lucky Feather off the balcony.

Then there's a knocking sound at the door.

"Who could that be?" Mom asks. Not Aunt Eira or Aunt Sorcha, I'm thinking, because they just walk in any time they come over. We do the same thing at their places. "Morley, get that, would you?" I see that she's got both her hands in a bowl of dough, so I put down my pencil and answer the door.

There's a police officer standing there. A man. "Uh, I'm looking for Ms. Star. Eefa. Is she at home?"

I turn to call mom to come to the door. The man comes into our front hallway.

"Constable Furness," he says. "From the regional police service. Can we talk …uh, privately?" he looks at me. "This won't take long."

Mom looks at me, as if I've done something wrong. "Go back to the kitchen, Morley," she says. "Call me when the timer goes off for the cookies."

She points the officer towards the living room, closing the door behind them. I'd like to know what they're talking about, but I head back to the kitchen, where Daisy is colouring with sparkle markers with one hand and eating one of the cookies that was on the cooling rack with the other.

I get back to work on my drawing and have almost forgotten about the police officer when mom comes back into the kitchen. He's right behind her.

The timer goes off and she takes the cookie sheet out of the oven. Then she turns and says, "Constable Furness is here because he wants to know about what you wrote in school. About a cat."

Constable Furness sits down at our kitchen table. "Hello Morley," he says. "You're not in any trouble at all. I just want to know about the kitten you...found. Can you tell me the story?" He pulls out a notebook and a pen from one of the many pockets on the thick belt he wears. I notice that his belt also has a two-way radio and wonder if it has a real gun.

Once again, I tell the story.

"And would you recognize this man again?" he says.

"Of course," I say. "He's the renter man who lives upstairs."

"Do you know his name?"

I don't, but my mother does. She tells him. He asks for any proof, and she says that they rented the upstairs, but always paid cash. She thinks she still has the rental agreement and goes to find it at the desk where she pays bills.

The officer says he'll write up these notes, and we may have to come down to the police station to make a formal statement and for my mother to sign it. He says that's because a kid can't swear to something that happened, even when it did. Their parent or guardian has to swear to it.

That seems kind of silly, because I hear kids swearing in the playground all the time.

Then he's gone and it's just the three of us in the kitchen with Daisy and me still drawing and mom still baking cookies. But the happiness is gone. Mom doesn't say anything, always a sign that she's getting angry but isn't ready to yell at me yet.

Later, after Daisy has fallen asleep but it's still an hour before my bedtime, I go out to the kitchen. I feel like I have to apologize to my mom, but I can't figure out what for. After all, the policeman said I did nothing wrong.

"Oh Morley, why couldn't you just leave well enough alone?" she says. I don't know what she means, so I don't say anything. I just poor myself a glass of milk and take three of the cookies for a bedtime snack.

"All this fuss about a cat. I don't understand it," she says, mostly to herself. "As if I don't have enough to worry about."

Worrying is something I understand. I'm in bed, listening to Daisy snorkel in her sleep, thinking about Feather and where he is and how he is right now.

Did the vet give him medicine?

Did his operation fix what was hurt?

Is he going to be OK?

When he is, can I get him back?

I try to talk to Feather in my mind, tell him I'm thinking about him and sending him hope to get better. But he must be too far away, or maybe asleep. Or maybe...

But I won't let myself think that.

Ever.

Feather IS alive and he's getting better and he's going to be OK.

And he's going to be mine and I will be his. What families are.

I know this. The wish bracelet for it broke.

That means it's going to happen.

fifteen

We don't know where this place is.

We don't know what illnesses those animals could have.

We don't know if people could catch something from the animals there and make you and your sister sick. And me. Especially now.

We can't take that risk, Morley...and I can't believe the police would come, for a cat...

Or so my mom says. These are her reasons for why we can't visit Feather at the pet shelter.

But I have to change her mind. Or just go, without getting permission. Because I REALLY need to know that Feather is going to be all right.

It's after school. Daisy has gone to play with her

friend Rachel.

I'm helping mom pack up for Saturday Market.

I've done a picture of Lucky Feather and put it in one of the picture frames we've fixed up. Under the picture, it says:

HELP ME HELP FEATHER!
Each bracelet sold
helps save pets
at Sunflower Pet Shelter.

My mother decided to let me put this up in our booth. I grab my favourite tin for keeping pencils in, the one that was a gift from Sam with Mackintosh's toffees in it, with the red tartan design on the top. Now, it's going to be my cash box for the pet shelter donations I collect at the Market.

I've been thinking about all her reasons for not going to the shelter. Mom is driving. Not saying anything.

"But it must be safe to go there because people do, all the time," I say.

"Hmmm?" Mom says. "Go where?"

"To the shelter. To adopt pets," I say. "And there's also the people that work there. And I know where it is." I know this not just because I was there with Mr. Maclean, but because our school bus passes right by the Sunflower Pet Shelter, on the days when I take the bus to school instead of going with mom and Daisy.

"Sam went there to get Tippy. And Mr. Maclean went there with me. So it must be safe, if they went there."

I know that Mr. Maclean is mom's boss. And also that she likes him. She says he'd "do anything for that poor little girl of his." She means Julia.

I've never told my mother about Julia punching me and calling names and all the other mean things she says and does. What would be the point? If my mom wants to feel sorry for Julia, because Julia's mother died, I can't stop her.

I know that's sad, but Julia is such a mean bully that I don't think she deserves being felt sorry for.

Even if she doesn't have a mother. She does have a father.

But I also know it's a waste of time even thinking about her. Maybe Mr. Maclean will change schools again and he'll have to move away and take bully Julia with him. He's not like his daughter at all. For a minute, I wonder how such a nice man could have such mean kid.

Aunt Eira says it does no good thinking like this. You have to take people as you find them, she says. This sounds kind of old school, but she says her mother always said that to her and to Eefa, who's my mom, and to their other sister, Sorcha. She says it's a true thing that it would be good for me to remember. Aunt Eira calls this a people skills tool.

Mom is silent the whole time I'm thinking all this. Finally, she sighs and says, "Well, I guess so."

"So we can go see Feather at the shelter? Maybe

today?"

"We'll see," she says, pulling into the grocery store's parking lot.

Hello Feather, I say in my mind. *I'm Morley. I'm the girl that picked you up and helped save you.*

I know he must be too far away to be able to hear me.

But soon, he won't be.

Soon, I hope, the Feather in my mind is going to be the kitten in my lap.

Or sitting on my desk, playing with my markers and trying to knock them on the floor when I'm drawing.

Or lying next to me on my bed, when I'm reading.

Or sitting in the window, washing his face with a paw and watching for us to get home from school.

I find some old cushions and put them on the window seat in front of our big window, the one that faces our driveway and the street. Ready to be what I know will be Lucky Feather's favourite place to sit in the sun and look out at birds and people and everything that's going on outside on Main Street.

I imagine him sitting there. The first time he sees birds. Or snow. Or stars in the sky.

I've stopped just wanting a pet. Or thinking about having a pet cat. Or wishing for a kitten.

The pet I wish for is Feather.

I know he's meant to join our family.

As I help my mother load groceries into the car, I

know in my heart that it's only a matter of time until Mom agrees.

And Danny. When he finally comes home.

sixteen

It's another good day at the Saturday Market.

A man who owns a restaurant asks if mom would make a birthday cake for his son. If he likes it, he says, he might add cakes as something they offer their restaurant guests.

And a couple of people buy bracelets and don't even take them! They say just sell them again and give that money to the pet shelter. People like that make me smile, every time I think about how generous they are.

More of the fancier bracelets sell than wish bracelets. The fancier ones have coloured beads and charms.

I've also made a few extra fairy bracelets, because Daisy liked them so I thought maybe there are other girls that like fairies. And sure enough, all those fairy bracelets sell the first hour we're at the market!

As mum says, in business you're always making more of your winners and less of the others. It's fun and interesting to guess what will sell and then see which types of cookies and which bracelets sell the fastest.

It isn't always the ones we think will sell right away! Which only goes to prove, mom says, that you just never know. You have to try things to see what works.

After the market, mom treats us to lunch at Fry Daddy's and then we go to the pet shelter.

"Now you understand, Morley, we're NOT coming home with a cat today," she says. "Or any other type of animal. But we can go there to see if that kitten is doing well. If you want, you can hand in the money you collected for them today. Or would you rather save it up and give them a bigger amount later?"

I don't know which would be better. I have $46 in my Mackintosh's toffee tin that people gave me today for the pet shelter. And more money, at home for the shelter, hidden in my room. Wouldn't it be better for them to get it right away?

Or should I wait till I save up more to give them all at once?

I wonder what Aunt Eira would say about this.

At the shelter, there's a woman at the front desk I've never seen here before. "Is this your first time here?" she says. "Are you here for a dog or a cat?"

"Yes," Mom says before I can answer. "It's our first time..."

"Well then, let me call someone to give you a tour." She turns back to her computer, and in a couple of minutes a man comes out from the back. Also someone I haven't met yet.

"Would it be the dogs or cats you're here to see?" He looks to my mother to answer, not me.

"It's Feather..." I say.

"Umm...cats, I think," Mom says.

"Our kitties are all in Room A and Room B," he says, pointing to the doors, one with a big A and the other with a B on them. "Wash your hands with warm water and soap at the sink. Then you can take a kitty out of the enclosure. Be sure to use hand sanitizer before you touch the next cat."

He turns away. That, I guess, is the whole tour.

Mom walks around, looking at cats in their tiny cages that are stacked up from the floor almost to the ceiling. She sticks her fingers into their cages and talks baby talk to them.

In each cage there could be one adult cat, or two, or several kittens, all in that cramped space. It is barely big enough for them to stand up and turn around.

Some of the cages are empty. And some have a card stuck on the front, telling the name and age of the kittens or cats inside and whether they're boys or girls.

I feel so sorry for all of them, stuck in these tiny little cages with just a litter pan, a food and water bowl and a scrap of towel to sit on. Poor them, just sitting there, waiting and waiting for someone to let them out and take them home. And, until then, not able to run around and play, like cats love to do.

I can't bear the thought of Feather being in one of these cages. Mom sits on a plastic chair, holding a little ginger kitten and exclaiming about how beautiful a pair of Siamese cats are. They're sharing the biggest cage.

I go out to the front desk.

"Excuse me," I say. "I need to know something."

The woman at the front, whose name tag says she's Tammie, keeps clicking away on her keyboard. "Hold on a sec..." she says.

I wait.

"Tammie! I need to know about Lucky Feather..."

"About a feather?" she says. "I don't know what you mean."

"This week. Mr. Maclean and I came here with a kitten. He was hurt. His name is Lucky Feather."

"And you surrendered this kitten?"

"Um, well..."

"You gave him to us. To look after. Was he a stray? Picked up by Animal Control?"

"He was hurt. Bad. He got thrown off a balcony." She looks shocked.

"By you?"

I could feel my bad mouth just getting ready to say something, when my mother says, "No, of course not. By people who live upstairs from us. My daughter and Mr. Maclean, who is principal of Seabright Primary, brought the kitten here on Wednesday."

"Oh, I see..." the woman says, starting to flip through some files on her desk. "Um, yes, here it is. Broken jaw, two broken ribs, other possible internal injuries, bruised kidney. The duty vet operated Wednesday evening...normal procedure...recovery normal...resting comfortably. About 10 weeks old, it says here...much too young to have left its mother..."

"Can I see him? Now?"

"That won't be possible, I'm afraid. He's still in recovery. Not available for adoption yet."

"How long will that take? You're sure he's getting better?"

"According to this, yes. But you can talk to one of the technicians...."

"No," Mom says. "I don't think that will be necessary. We need to get back. It's just about time to pick up Daisy."

"Wait!" I say. "Just tell me, when will he be ready to be adopted?"

Mom has already walked towards our car. But I know she won't leave without me.

"Could be a while. I can't say. You'd have to talk to the vet. Sorry. Why don't you check back in a week? There'll be more in his file by then."

I sigh. More waiting. And the whole time I've been here, I've been trying to hear Feather in my mind. But he must be sleeping right now, because he doesn't answer.

I simply can't wait a whole week.

I have to know.

After school the next day I ride my bike to the pet shelter. I know it's Dr. Van Haan's day to be there.

Tammie doesn't want to interrupt the vet, but I insist and finally, she phones someone. Almost right away, Jayden's mom comes out to talk to me.

We sit for a minute on those hard plastic chairs in the front lobby.

Feather is doing well. Better than expected, Dr. Van Haan says. He had serious injuries, but he is an otherwise healthy kitten and he has every chance to survive.

She thanks me for doing the right thing.

But there's no more she can say, yet. And no, I'm not allowed to see him. Though she'll take a picture with her phone and send it to Jayden to show me tomorrow at school.

It's less than I want, but for now, it has to be enough.

A few days later, Aunt Eira picks me up from school and we collect Daisy from her afternoon daycare. We go back to our aunt's apartment. While Daisy is doing a fairy puzzle, Aunt Eira asks about what's new and interesting in my life.

I tell her more about Feather. She already knows the first part of this story. I tell her about getting all the donations for the shelter from people at the market.

And saving them in my toffee tin hidden under my

bed.

And about how we went to the shelter, but I forgot to hand in the money.

And how there were a lot of kittens and cats in those awful cages. But I didn't get to see Lucky Feather. But then Doctor Van Haan told me about his operation and sent me a picture of him.

And how badly I want to adopt him.

"OK," my aunt says. "Well, I see where you need two things. ONE is a bank account, to put your earnings in and the donation money. I'll suggest your mum take you to open a bank account. And TWO is you need to go visit Feather. So, let's do that."

"Now?"

"Of course now. Get your coat and call Daisy. I'll text your mom that you're staying for dinner and I'll bring you home by bedtime."

At the pet shelter, all Daisy wants to do is sit in the lobby and colour a pet picture the desk lady gives her along with a little paper cup of crayons.

All I want to do is see Feather. Even though I know I probably can't, yet.

All Aunt Eira wants to do is see everything there.

Tammie is on the front desk again, but she doesn't recognize me. She calls someone out, and they tell us all about Room A and Room B and the hand sanitizer and my aunt just smiles and they leave us to look in the cages.

My aunt opens one with a little silvery-gray kitten with a striped tail and cuddles her. "Oh, you are so sweet," she says.

I'm sort of pretending to look around. Really, I'm listening for Feather.

I'm here now, I say in my head. *I hope your ribs don't hurt any more and you can breathe. And your jaw is better, so you can eat.*

*Soft...*he says. *Warm...Close. Near. Kind girl.*

Don't worry, I tell him in my mind. *The people here are taking care of you. And then you can come home. With me.*

But Feather is not coming home with us today. He's not ready to be adopted yet.

Instead, the little gray kitten is. Aunt Eira says she's irresistible and she's adopting her.

Daisy and I wait while our aunt fills out some papers and promises to always take her new pet to the vet and to give her loving care.

The shelter has already given the kitten her kitten shots to protect from cancer and other illnesses and she's been neutered. That means she won't ever have babies. They do this because there are already too many pets waiting for good homes in pet shelters.

It is $200 to adopt a kitten. Aunt Eira pulls out a credit card to pay.

$200 is a lot of money. I know I have that much saved up from Christmas and birthday money and also from selling bracelets, but mom is probably going to say I can't use that money to get Lucky Feather.

And I know that I'm the one that brought Feather here to the shelter, but that doesn't count. He wasn't mine when I found him. He belonged to the renters. But they lost him when they abused him and threw him away.

He belongs to the shelter now.

Even though in my heart, he's mine. Forever.

And I still have no idea how he's going to be mine, forever.

Mom says we've still got a No Pets Rule. Because pets cost money and make noise and damage the furniture and smell and a bunch of other reasons. Or excuses.

Aunt Eira is signing her name and paying and waiting for the shelter people to go get her kitten and collecting the little bag of cat food they give you with every cat adopted.

Daisy is getting restless. I've shown her the cat rooms, but she isn't interested. She wants to know if we're going to Mickey Dees for dinner. That's her favourite place because they've got pink milkshakes.

I'm sort of listening to what the woman is saying to Aunt Eira, and looking around the room and at posters on the wall. One of them tells about the shots pets need and when and what disease each shot helps prevent. Another poster says the pet shelter needs volunteers.

I take a volunteer application form from the holder on the wall next to the poster. It says to look on their website for more information about Volunteer Opportunities. I can't wait to get back to Aunt Eira's to go online and find out what this means. Because if I can be a volunteer here, then I can see Lucky Feather. And know he's OK.

Just until he comes home with me.

One of the technicians comes out with a cardboard carry box with Aunt Eira's little gray kitten inside.

I wish it was Lucky Feather.

But I'm happy for my aunt. And for Sheena. That's the shelter name for this little kitten she's adopting.

"What's that you've got?" Eira says.

"It's about volunteering."

"Yes, we couldn't care for the animals without our wonderful volunteers," Tammie says. "Are you interested in volunteering?" she asks Eira, still ignoring me.

My aunt is helping Daisy into her coat. "No, at least not right now. But Morley here is."

"Ah, that's too bad. Volunteers need to be 16 or older."

"Oh..." I say. "But isn't there something...?"

"Well, maybe. Could you come and be one of our cat cuddlers? We always have poor little kitties that need some attention...that is, if it's OK with your mother."

"Cat cuddling. Yes, I think that could be OK," Eira says.

"Well, fill out the application and bring it back in and we'll see," the woman says.

Maybe she's really nicer than I thought she was.

"Don't worry about your mom," Eira says to me on the way back to her place. That's after we get take-out meals and stop at the pet store to get a litter pan, scooper, litter and more kitten food along with some cat treats and cat toys. The gray kitten sits all the way in the back corner of the box and doesn't make a sound.

I wonder if she's scared about what's happening.

Or worried about who these strangers are.

Or where we're going. And what's going to happen to her next.

But I can't hear anything in my head that this kitten is thinking.

As soon as we get to Eira's place, she says we can open the carry box and touch the kitten. Very gently.

But the kitten runs away and hides. We don't see where. Daisy and I search and search through every room in Eira's apartment. We look under the bed and behind the couch and in the closets. We can't find her.

That's OK, my aunt says. She'll come out when she's ready. It's just really frightening for a new little pet, being in a different place with people she doesn't know.

It must be like that for Feather, too, I think.

I expect we'll get home to find out our mother had a

nice peaceful evening, what she's always saying she wants, but no. She's baking and crying. I'm suddenly afraid to find out what awful thing has happened.

It's Eira who sends Daisy off to get into her pajamas, with me to help her, while Eira makes hot drinks and sits my mother down to talk.

I'm helping Daisy, but I'm also half listening. As much as I can.

It's the upstairs renters.

They're gone.

Fantastic, I think. This is incredible news. No more awful swearing and screaming and fights and clomping around.

No more of that horrid man who hurts people. And pets.

And maybe now we can have the upstairs back. I'll get my own room back. Daisy will get hers. So will mom.

But clearly, my mom doesn't think this is good at all. It's like the worst thing that could happen.

I don't understand.

I bring Daisy out to the kitchen to get her bedtime hot chocolate. Then I'll read her a bedtime story. Or maybe mom will.

But it turns out mom has gone from sad and crying to angry. With ME!

"If it wasn't for that damned CAT!" she says. "Morley, really, I can't believe that you could cause so much trouble..."

"No," Eira is saying. "You don't mean that, Eefa, surely. It isn't Morley's fault"

I don't know what to say. I wasn't the one who made the renters go away. Even if it is a good thing that they're gone.

"Oh, Morley, you stupid girl!"

"No, Eefa. No.," my aunt says, "Morley isn't that at all. Now, let's see what we can do…"

"Do? Do? We can't do anything. They're gone. They didn't pay their rent. Now they're gone. And I don't know…"

"We call the police," Eira says. "But first, we make sure they didn't take anything valuable with them."

We all look around to see if anything is missing.

It is.

My money from selling bracelets is gone. Under my bed, I find the red toffee tin where I keep the pet shelter donation money. Now it's all bent up. And empty.

I thought I had it really carefully hidden, but I guess not.

Some antique candle holders are gone from the bookcase in the living room. They're ones that mom got from her grandmother. They're silver and probably valuable.

And money my mother hid in one of her old purses is also gone. And food from the fridge and some of my mother's clothes. And some things Danny left here.

That's bad. But then we go upstairs, and my mother gasps and starts to cry again.

The whole place is trashed.

Furniture is turned over.

The windows are left wide open.

The heat is blasting out, turned all the way up.

It smells like someone was smoking. There are burn marks on the floors.

There are a couple of holes punched in the wall of the bedroom.

The toilet and bathtub look like nobody's cleaned them. Ever. They stink.

And the whole place smells like garbage and dirty diapers.

"Oh God," my mom says. "Oh my dear God..."

Aunt Eira takes over.

She sends Daisy and me around to close all the open windows. She turns down the heat. She leads our mother downstairs. She calls the police.

Long after I get Daisy to bed, long after my aunt helps my mother to her bed, long after Aunt Eira calls a friend to stop by her place and look after her new kitten, long after she goes to sleep on the couch in the living room...long after our house gets quiet, I lay awake, looking at the skinny moon out the window and thinking about how all this might be my fault. Is it?

Or is it Danny's fault? It might not have happened if he didn't leave.

Or is it my mom's fault? She let those renters into our house. Why did she let bad people move in here and not pay the rent?

Or is it just those renters' fault? They're the ones who made the mess and did the damage and stole from us and hurt Feather.

The next day, I'm so tired from all these questions I just about fall asleep in class. Mrs. Green sends me to the principal's office.

Again.

Mr. Maclean asks me why I'm so tired I can't stay awake.

So I tell him. Because you don't tell lies when the principal asks you to explain your behaviour.

What would be the point? He'd just find out anyways.

I expect him to tell me to be a sensible girl and go to bed earlier because you can't learn anything if you don't get your rest and blah-blah-blah.

He doesn't say any of that.

seventeen

It's a week later.

And it seems like our house is full of people. A lot of them are the grade 10s from the shops and carpentry course at Horton High School. The teacher there is a friend of Mr. Maclean's and the grade 10s have to do a volunteer project. It turns out our house is their project.

They've helped gather all the trash and fix the holes in the walls and, since we're doing all this, Eira says, why don't we put in bathrooms for the other bedrooms up here? The insurance money should cover it. Dom has a friend who does that kind of work.

Mom is kind of going around in a daze. Sometimes she's upstairs helping, but mostly she's down in the kitchen, making sandwiches and cakes and cookies and coffee and tea for all the volunteers.

It's a miracle, she says.

Even Officer Furness comes to help, when he's off duty.

So does Mr. Maclean.

And Eira's boyfriend, Dom.

And Jayden. And his brother, Patrick.

And Sam. And Sam's Tia Margaret.

Daisy even helps, a little bit.

In just a few days, the whole mess is gone. All the walls are freshly painted and Aunt Eira has taken some of mom's furniture finds from the garage and some things from her place and bought some things and it looks – nice.

Fresh. Clean.

Like home.

But we aren't moving back upstairs.

Mom is looking for new renters. But, she says, she's learned her lesson. She's going to make absolutely sure the next people are responsible.

"Why not do a bed-and-breakfast?" Aunt Sorcha says one day when we're taking a break. "There's so many tourists looking for a nice, clean, homey place to stay. And you're right on Main Street, close to everything. Why don't you do that?"

My mom looks stunned. Like she never, ever thought of doing a bed-and-breakfast.

Even though her friend Marielle has summer tourists renting her spare bedroom, ever since her daughter went to university and then wanted her own place.

"But how do you...?" Mom says.

"It's all online now, you know," Eira says. "You put up some pictures and a description of what you've got which is, let's see, four bedrooms, each with its own full bathroom. Spacious family home with garden. Convenient parking. Close to restaurants, theatre, hiking trails and white sand beaches. Includes continental breakfast with home-baked cookies, scones and local jams..."

"Wow," Mr. Maclean says. "If I didn't already have a house, I'd want to stay here."

My mom just looks dazed. "Well...I guess. How do you start?"

And just like that, we take some photos, Aunt Eira and Dom put our listing on the internet and, two days later, our very first guest arrives. With their puppy.

Because, as Eira pointed out, there aren't many places for people travelling with their pets to stay in or even near our town. And who'd bother travelling with a pet that doesn't behave?

I could have fallen right off my chair when my mom said, "Well, I guess so. We could try it."

There aren't a lot of tourists yet, but there will be soon, just like every summer. Our town always gets really busy by June and stays busy, almost up to Thanksgiving. Like my mom says, we're really lucky to live here, in our pretty little town near the ocean. A lot of people visit. A lot more wish they could.

Soon there isn't a night when we don't have guests upstairs.

Mom is still baking. We're still selling bracelets and baked goods at the market together. And I'm helping her with the bed-and-breakfast guests. My jobs are vacuuming and dusting and helping change the beds and scrub the bathtubs. She says it's just too hard to do all this, for one person.

The amazing thing is mom is paying me to help out.

AND she agreed that I shouldn't have to try to hide my money in our room. So one day, after school, we go to the bank and she signs some papers so I can have my own bank account for my bracelets business and the pet shelter donation money. That's just to keep it safe until I give it to the pet shelter to help the animals.

Because now I have to work extra hard to be able to make up the pet shelter donation money that the renters stole. Even though it wasn't my fault, it feels like something I have to do.

And I need to earn money for Feather.

Mom says I've been such a help to her, with Daisy and with the upstairs fix-up and the guests and the cookie business, that as long as I still help out and keep my grades up at school, I have her permission to volunteer at the pet shelter.

I'm so excited, I can hardly wait to tell Jayden and Sam that part of my Get A Pet plan is already working!

eighteen

"You're a kind and brave girl to have rescued the kitten, Morley" Dr. Ifan says, when I'm introduced to him. "I wish more young people had your empathy for animals!"

There are 15 of us at the Volunteer Welcome night at the pet shelter. Right now, Dr. Ifan is talking to us about pet health. He's already thanked all of us for what he calls our "dedication to animal welfare."

He doesn't know that there's one particular animal here I care the most about.

He turns back to the table where there is a huge and hairy Main Coon cat and gives him a needle while one of the technicians holds him.

What Dr. Ifan is saying is interesting and useful to know, but I'm only half listening because I'm looking everywhere for Feather.

And listening for him.

I know Feather has to be here somewhere, probably in a little cage and probably asleep right now because I can't hear him in my mind.

Then I hear it, very faintly: *Girl. Girl. Safe.*

It has to be Feather!

"*Yes,*" I say to him in my head. "*I'm Morley. I brought you here.*"

"*Bad place. Dogs. Smells. Hurt.*"

"*A bad man hurt you. People here help you.*"

A few of the other volunteers are teenagers, but mostly they're grown-ups. I hoped the vet talking to us might be Jayden's mom, but this isn't her day to be here.

And I know I'm not a real volunteer, because I'm not 16. I like to think I'm a junior volunteer, but they don't have them. Right now, they're just letting me tag along with the group and, maybe, help out some.

But I know in my heart that this is a place I want to be, helping kittens and cats. And maybe dogs too. They're all like Feather. Hurt and alone and afraid of what's happening to them. Needing a home where people care for them and love them.

Helping the animals feels like an important thing to do.

I don't think you need to be a grown-up to do important things.

On this tour for new volunteers, we've seen everything anyone could come here and see. That's

Room A and Room B with the cats in cages and the kitty lounge where sometimes cats are let out to play on the climbing towers.

The dogs are kept in the back and you have to see their picture, posted out front. Then if you think you might adopt a dog, you have to apply to be allowed to meet them.

Tammie, who has taken over leading our tour, says that they have far fewer dogs than cats at this shelter. She doesn't say why. No one asks.

All I want to ask is where is Feather. Or Shane, as I've found out the shelter people call him. A stupid name, I think, but Feather probably doesn't care.

Want home, Feather says.

I hang back from the group to snoop. Behind what looks like a closet door, there's a little room, like a broom closet. It has six cages in it. Three cages have cats in them. All these cats have bandages and places where their fur has been shaved off.

"No, close that door, please. That's our care room for cats recovering from surgery. It's off limits to everyone except the vet and technicians," one of the pet assistants says.

But what's still wrong with Feather? Why is he still recovering? Why hasn't he healed yet? And how can I find out? I think of asking Jayden's mother.

All I know is that right now Feather is in the place for recovering. That means he must be getting better. Not worse.

Feather, you're getting better, I say silently to him. *And when you're all the way better, you'll be coming home with me. People here care about you getting healthy, and I care the most.*

He doesn't answer, just yawns and goes back to sleep.

Sleep is good. We did a unit about sleep in grade four, so I know that when you sleep, your body fights illness. That's also when your body does its growing.

And why, when you don't sleep, you get sicker.

"Sleep little Feather. Get well and strong," I whisper to myself as we're led back out to the front and the tour ends. We all say thank you and everybody writes down their names and phone numbers and e-mail addresses and says when they'll come and volunteer. I don't have an e-mail address so I put in Aunt Eira's.

We're all told that we'll get a message about what volunteer jobs we will do but I already know what I'll be doing. Cuddling cats.

Helping clean their cages and fill their food and water bowls. Helping the other volunteers with whatever they're doing that day.

Taking pictures of the cats to put on the website.

That's what I've offered to do. My mom signed the papers that say she's given her permission.

I don't tell anyone this, but I'm hoping soon they let me do more.

All week I make bracelets and help mom with her baking. We sell everything, or just about all of it, every Saturday at the market. Sunday is the day for church, on the days my mother says she has the energy to go, and then to relax.

Sundays are also the day I spend all afternoon at the pet shelter. It's my favourite time of the whole week. Each week, Feather is a bit better, but he's still pretty grumpy about the getting better part.

I know what that feels like. The whole time I was home getting better, I was grumpy about having to do that instead of just having my regular life, the one where I didn't have a cast on my arm and sore ribs so it hurt to laugh.

I go to the pet shelter every chance I get. Every time I'm there, I try to cheer him up.

I promise that soon, he'll be coming home with me.

And then it's June 10, and the first happy thing about summer, because that's Sam's Birthday Party.

Even though it's a Saturday, I get to go to her party because Aunt Eira does Saturday market that day with mom and Daisy.

It turns out we were so confused about all of Sam's hints about her epic birthday party because she's having two parties. First, there's a sleep-over party, for girls only.

Jayden looks really disappointed when he hears this.

But he brightens up a bit when Sam says that then, the next day, there's a big backyard pool party for all the kids in grade five, boys and girls.

And the theme, she says, is her mom's idea. It's going to be a Hawaii Luau party, with a real pig roast, and hula dancing lessons and a fire show in the evening for all the parents as well as the kids.

Sam always has the best parties. She's so excited that Jayden and I get really excited, too.

I can hardly wait!

nineteen

All my favourite people, or almost all of them, are crowded into our living room.

Mom and Eira have already passed around the cookies and gotten everyone drinks of coffee or tea, or cranberry juice for the kids.

Now they're all sitting and waiting for me to start talking. I've got my posters set up and my notes. Eira and Dom helped me make my presentation slides. Eira's running the slides with her laptop and projecting them up on the wall.

Sam and Jayden are smiling their encouragement.

Daisy is the only one not paying attention, but I expected that. At least she's being quiet, for once.

What I didn't expect is that something feels like it's squeezing my throat closed. And my mouth is really, really dry.

I take a sip of juice, but it doesn't seem to help.

It's strange, because I know exactly what I'm going to say.

I practiced in front of the bathroom mirror about a dozen times.

Then I did the whole thing for just Jayden and Sam. They liked it and had some great ideas about how to make my presentation better.

I know I'm ready. I glance down at my notes.

But suddenly, I feel all sweaty, like the room is too hot.

Then I start, and it's like there's someone talking too fast in this high, squeaky voice that doesn't sound like me at all.

But I figure I better keep going. And try to slow down. And talk more like me.

I pause.

Smile.

Start again.

Everybody is looking at me. They mostly look interested.

So I keep going.

Because they expect me to. Some of them even want me to.

I tell them why kids need pets.

And why pets need kids.

And what you need to do to get ready to have a pet.

And how much they cost for adopting them and their food and going to the vet and everything else they need.

And what it means to be a responsible pet owner.

And ways kids who get a pet can help pay for their pet. That's by doing chores or using their allowance or maybe starting a business, like me making and selling jewellery at the market. There are lots of ways to earn money for your pet.

I talk about how to know which pet is best for you. Or not right for you at all.

And how you could go to a pet breeder to find your pet, but also how there are so many good pets just waiting for a kind home at the pet shelters.

I talk about how pets can live for a long time, with good care. So you need to be really sure you want them, because they're a family member. And they depend on you for everything.

Their whole lives depend on you.

My presentation doesn't have everything I learned about in the Get A Pet project I did with Jayden and Sam. I learned a lot more about having a cat, like what things are poison to them that you can't ever let them eat.

And why you need to check that their ears and teeth are clean.

And how to trim their claws so it doesn't hurt them. It's just like cutting your fingernails. If you cut too short, it will hurt.

But this presentation isn't about EVERYTHING there is to know about pets. It's about the basic things you need to know before you get a pet.

Everyone claps their hands when I finish.

Jayden says, "That was incredible! There was stuff in there I didn't know and our family has lots of pets!"

Sam says, "You should do this at school. I bet you'd get an A for it!"

Eira says, "Well, I filmed the whole thing. That was really good!"

"Especially the slides!" Dom says. "And the drawings! We should turn those into infographics and post them online!"

"So, does this mean we're getting a dog or a cat?" Daisy says. For once, she's saying what I'm thinking.

"Well, I guess we'll have to see…" Mom says. "But that was a very good presentation, Morley. Very thorough. Everyone could hear you. And you didn't talk for too long. Well done!"

And then everyone is laughing and talking and getting up to leave.

"Don't worry," Sam says to me. "She's going to say, 'Yes.' I know it."

I know that, too. I just wish it was right now.

Darla, the nice woman at the shelter, said it looks like Shane – but she really means Feather - could be ready to be adopted in another couple of weeks. That means two weeks. Or three. I want to have everything ready for him.

Mom doesn't know, but I've already bought a litter box and food dish and a bag of cat litter and a bag of kitten food. They were kind of heavy to get home with my bike, but I did. And I even managed to get them inside without anyone noticing. All Feather's supplies are hidden in a corner of our basement that nobody ever goes to.

At the shelter, I ask if I can put dibs on Lucky Feather, so no one else can get him. But they say that isn't possible. You need to apply for a pet and, if they're a cat, you can adopt them the same day.

You just can't prevent someone else from adopting the exact one you want before you can.

This means I HAVE to find a way to get my mom to say we can have a cat.

Thinking about the day that she says, "OK" and we go get Feather and bring him home fills me with that happy feeling, like it's my birthday and Christmas morning and the best day at the beach and I've just done the best drawing of my entire life, all rolled up in one explosion of total joy.

It's a few days later when Mrs. Green gets a message that I'm wanted at the principal's office.

I wonder what I've done this time.

My mother sends me her worried 'What have you done this time?' look when I get to the office. "You can go right in," she says. "He's waiting!"

But Mr. Maclean doesn't look annoyed. He's smiling. He stands up and even reaches out to shake my hand.

"Congratulations, Morley," he says. "This is really wonderful!"

I wonder what he's talking about.

He turns his computer screen so we can both see it. He plays a video that's on YouTube. I'm surprised to see that it's me, talking about how to get ready to have a pet.

Then I see there are other videos there of me! All are other parts of my presentation. And every video has an advertisement on it at the beginning, about buying a family car or pet food or getting pet insurance.

"I don't understand," I say, thinking about how my presentation got there and there are already views and likes.

"I didn't either, at first," Mr. Maclean says. "But I thought your Aunt Eira and Uncle Dom might have something to do with it. So I called them. And your mother, of course. And I called the Sunflower Pet Shelter to see what they know."

Really? Why, I wondered.

Mr. Maclean points to a sentence underneath each video. It says that all proceeds are being donated to the Sunflower Pet Shelter in Seabright. "Proceeds" means money.

Wow! Incredible! Is this the surprise Eira promised me for my passing-Grade-5 present this year? If so, it's totally awesome! Unbelievable!

It must have been Eira and Dom who put those videos online.

Best. Gift. EVER!

The only thing that could be better is handing Feather to me. For keeps. But I know I'm the one who has to do the work to make that wish happen.

But this – using my presentation to help all the animals at the shelter – this is really making me smile.

I'm pleased. And proud.

"So I was wondering, Morley. How would you feel about repeating your presentation for other students here at school? Maybe the last week of school, when we usually have presentations and movies..."

"And parties..."

"Well, yes. And parties. But before school ends, I think a lot of kids would enjoy and really learn from this presentation of yours, which I've learned more about from your aunt. And your mother, of course..."

My mother. She still doesn't want me to have a pet. Will she let me tell other kids about having pets? Suddenly, my happiness starts to slip away.

"Your mother agrees with me that it's an excellent idea."

Well, that's a surprise.

Or maybe that was what was really happening.

Maybe my mother was just *pretending* to have the No Pets Rule, but really, I'm getting Feather for a passing-Grade 5 present from her. And Danny.

Or for my birthday, which is in July. Next month.

That must be it!

Once I think about it, it all makes so much sense!

Suddenly, I'm so excited, I just about want to burst. I have to tell someone. And then pretend to be really surprised when I actually GET Feather.

I can do that.

"Yes," I tell Mr. Maclean. "I can do that."

Which is how, the second-to-last week of school, I do my Get A Pet presentation for all the grade threes.

Other teachers hear about it, so then I do my presentation again for all the grade fours.

And then one for all the grade fives. And even Mrs. Green, who says she's allergic to pet dander, says the presentation was "well-researched and well-presented."

But the real surprise is how happy the people are at the pet rescue shelter. They say they know how much money it's making from the advertising, because Dom called them and told them all about it. Already, it's one of their best fund-raisers. That means they're getting money they need to help the animals.

I feel really good about this. Not just that it's helping Feather and hurt pets like him, but all the homeless cats and dogs and rabbits and birds and other pets the shelter helps go to good homes where people love them.

I was riding home on my bike one Sunday afternoon, going the back way along the rail walking trail because it's the fastest way home, when suddenly, Julia was there, blocking the path.

Usually, on a beautiful day like this, there'd be lots of people out jogging or with kids in strollers or walking their dogs. But there doesn't seem to be anyone in sight.

Which is bad, when you come up against a bully.

"Hey tall, dark and stupid!" Julia says, knocking my lucky hat off my head.

None of these things are true about me. I'm not tall, I have red hair and I do OK in school, so I know I'm not stupid.

"Talking about yourself again?" I ask her. Which, now that I think about it, is all true, but was probably a dumb thing to say. I should have just ignored her.

Or turned it into a joke, somehow.

Or said something like, "What? I can't hear you. What did you say?"

Or just have kept going and gotten away from her.

Now, I wish I had.

"You think you're so special, which is just sad. That pet thing you did was really stupid. 'Ooooh, I just want a pet, whaa, whaa, whaa,'" she said in her fake-y high voice, like a crying baby. "Bet you know that everybody's laughing at you?"

I know that isn't true. Julia is such a liar.

"And that dumb pet place you like to go to..." but how does she know where I go? Is she following me? That isn't just bullying. It's stalking.

"Well, you know that the animals that don't get adopted, they just get rid of them. The ones that nobody wants to buy?"

No, I didn't know this. "It isn't true!" I say. "And you're not buying the animals. You're paying for the care they get until you adopt them. They look after them there. They're really good people."

"No, they don't, you dummy. They let people see them and if nobody buys them right away, they just kill them!"

I'd like to hit her, as if that would make her stop saying such horrible things. She's laughing.

Then some dog walkers come along the path.

Julia shoves me, too hard, on my hurt arm, steps on my hat and says, "Hey, see ya around, crybaby," and she's gone.

I know Julia's a mean girl.

I know she makes things up. Horrible things.

I know I shouldn't be standing here, on the rail path, bawling my eyes out. One of the dog walkers comes over to see if I'm all right.

"Um...yeah. Fine," I say, grabbing my hat, getting back on my bike and heading home.

The next day at recess I get some good news.

Jayden's mom has texted to say that Feather is

recovering well. Just the way he should. He's going to be a healthy cat soon, she says.

It helps me feel better but doesn't wipe away how awful Julia is. The things she said.

Just telling my friends what happened is making me want to cry again. I'm trying not to.

"Don't ever listen to her! And don't let her get to you! She's just such a liar," Jayden says. "That's what bullies are. They tell lies to get attention. Because they're so sad and messed up, all they know how to do is hurt and be haters."

Jayden pulls out the phone he got for his birthday and sends another text to his mom. Amazingly, she answers almost right away. She says the Sunflower shelter is a No-Kill shelter. This means they care for every animal until it gets a home. That's unless they're so sick or badly hurt that nothing can save them.

"Sadly, some shelters don't save all the animals they could," Jayden's mum says.

That's not any shelter she'd volunteer at.

I didn't know Jayden's mom is a volunteer.

That's interesting.

I decide to make a drawing for her. A Thank You drawing. An Every Pet Gets A Home drawing.

The next day, I'm over at Aunt Eira's with Daisy. Daisy is playing with Pixel. That's what she and Dom are calling their new kitten. Pixel looks a little bit like Feather, but she is totally gray except for her white paws and a patch of white on her chest. And her gray striped tail.

Aunt Eira shows me some things on her laptop. We look at the videos on YouTube. They've got a lot more views and likes now. Then she shows me the Sunflower Pet Shelter website. Dom is designing a new one for them, she says. She wants to know what I think should be on the website. Like I'm a grown-up and I have thoughts and ideas that are worth listening to.

That's the special thing about Eira. She treats me like a person. Not just a kid.

Then we talk about my bracelet business. I still sell some of the wish bracelets to kids at school, for $2 each. They cost very little to make and only take about five minutes to do each one. But mostly, I sell more of the fancier bracelets at the market. Some people have asked me to make earrings, or necklaces, to match my bracelet designs.

And more people are asking me to do pet portraits.

We look at how much money I've made and put in the bank. Eira can do this online, too. It's amazing how many things you can do with a computer. I'm excited to learn this. She says it will be very useful in life as well as in my jewellery business. I think it's really interesting.

Then we look at Eira's blog. It's called DIVA Delish! It's all about being young and stylish and having fun but not spending a lot of money. There's beauty tips and things about clothing and doing your hair and how to put on a party. There's also how to work from home, like Eira does and how to start a small business, like my jewellery business or mom's baking business.

Basically, it's all the things in Eira's life – the vintage clothes she likes and where she gets them, the gifts she makes or buys for people, getting her kitten, how to have a great vacation close to home that doesn't cost a lot of money, ways to have fun on a date for less than $25 …stuff like that for teenagers and what she calls twenty-somethings. That means people who are older than 20, but not 30 yet. People like Eira. And her boyfriend, Dom.

She says she's just about sold out of all the bracelets I made to sell on her website. And could I make more, but this time she wants them with beads and chain or wire. She says she'll drive me to the big craft store in the city or we can look online for supplies. I say, "How about we do both?" and she laughs.

And, she says, she's found some instructions for how to make the kind of bracelets she wants to sell. She says she found them online.

She asks if I'd do exclusive designs? That means, I don't sell them anywhere else except on her website. They'll be my designs. With my name on them.

I'm thrilled!

twenty

Finally, it's the last day of school.

The other classes are having a big party. Mrs. Green says we don't go to school to have parties. We're at school to learn, she says, not to eat cupcakes.

So we watch movies about saving the Northern Right Whales and what to do in case of a forest fire like they're having out West and in Australia this year and what kids can do about climate change because the polar ice is melting and stuff like that.

But after lunch, Mrs. Green surprises us. She's brought a sheet cake so big everybody gets seconds, and she pours out paper cups of juice.

Everybody gets a little bag of candies and a book as a gift, chosen especially for them.

She says it's been a pleasure and an honour to teach

us, and all the other kids she's taught for the last 42 years. She says she'll miss teaching. She says this is her very last day, as a teacher. Because, after this, she's going to retire.

At recess, we talk about what we're going to do this summer. Jayden says he'll ride Spirit and help exercise the other horses and do all the other jobs there are to do. He'll work in their farm greenhouses, like he always does.

Jayden is excited about earning money this summer because he really wants to take scuba diving lessons. And he wants a camera that can take pictures underwater. He's saving up his summer wages, he says.

And his parents are taking him on a road-trip. Out to Vancouver. That'll take up most of July.

Sam says she still has to practice piano three hours a day and violin two hours a day, just like she always does. But she's going out to Jayden's place on Saturdays to learn how to ride horses. His brother Patrick is teaching her. She says her mom finally said she could. She's getting riding lessons as one of her birthday gifts.

And she said that she and her mom will be gone for most of the summer. They're going to France. Then Italy. I don't know anything about those places, but I guess we will, when Sam tells us about her summer.

I'm going to have more time for drawing and painting. And making bracelets. And helping my mom with her baking. And selling at the market. And doing pet portraits.

Soon, there will be lots of tourists, which just means we'll have guests for the bed-and-breakfast every single night, mom says. And we'll sell even more stuff at the market.

She says I should prepare to be busier than we ever were in the springtime. But, she promises, no matter how busy we get, there'll still be time to go to the beach and get ice creams and go hiking and do the other fun summer stuff we always do. Mom, Daisy and me.

She doesn't say anything about Danny doing any of the summer fun things with us.

I think about my Get Danny Home project. I have almost nothing done. I don't know where he is, so I can't write to him and ask him to come home.

And I don't know when Feather will come home.

Mom doesn't say anything when I talk about summer vacation being a good time to get a pet because you're home and have more time to help them get settled in your family than during the school year.

I want to spend more time at the pet shelter. I've done a lot of cat-cuddling and getting food and water bowls refilled and cleaning out litter boxes.

I've even learned how to take the dogs for walks.

I also take pet pictures to post on the website about available pets.

I did the artwork for posters for the Spring Pet Fling dinner to raise money for the shelter.

I love it that they don't call me the "helper" any more.

They call me "one of the volunteers," even though I'm the youngest one.

Something I don't talk about, not even to Jayden and Sam, is that Danny might come to visit this summer. We just don't know when yet. But Daisy is really excited. It seems like a long time since we've seen him.

I wonder if he's going to move back to be with us. Or if it's just a visit.

And how I'll feel about that. When it happens. Because it's odd, but right now, I don't really miss him. Not as much as I did.

Does my mom feel the same? I don't ask her. We just aren't a family that talks about stuff like that.

One day in July, I notice that mom is getting, not fat exactly, but sort of chubby. In the middle. And in her face. Also, she walks differently, sort of leaning back on her heels. And, this is strange, her blonde hair is suddenly really shiny. And she's always doing things. She has a lot of energy.

Almost like a little kid. Like Daisy.

And, this is the oddest thing, she asks me what I think about things.

"What things?" I say.

"Well, like the end of school. Summer vacation. Danny..."

I don't know what she wants me to say. I'm not even sure what I really think. I end up not saying anything.

She's sorry, she says, for being so short-tempered with me. And impatient. And what she calls "leaning on me too much." I think that means she makes me do too much work and not have enough time to just be a kid.

"And crabby," I say.

"Yes, that too."

She says she sometimes forgets that I'm only 10.

"Almost 11," I say. "Which is old enough to be home alone. And be a responsible pet owner.

"So, do you think we could go get Feather? Maybe today?" I already know from the shelter people that he's healthy, he's had all his shots and he's been neutered, so he won't ever make any babies. In just a few more days, he'll be in Room A for adoption. That means, ready to come home. With me.

"Well...um. Maybe," Mom says, with the sort of dreamy look on her face that I see Daisy do all the time. Right now, with her hair pulled back in a ponytail, our mother looks just like a grown-up copy of Daisy.

I've got a ponytail too, but I have lots of curly red hair, not straight hair like them. And my eyes are blue, not blue-green like Daisy's, or almost violet like mum's. I look nothing like them. Or like anyone in our family. Which has always made me wonder if I'm adopted.

When I was maybe about as old as Daisy is now, I asked mum about if I'm adopted. She just laughed and said no, I was 100 per cent hers. That means totally.

But what about my father? My real one? I know Danny isn't my father, because I remember the time before he came to live with us, when I was five.

All she's ever said about my real father is he was just someone she used to know. They were together, she said, but it didn't work out. I don't know what this means. Or what his name is. Or what he looks like. I've never even seen a photo of him.

I don't know why he never comes to visit. Or never writes to me. Or never even sends a birthday card.

"It's going to be a good summer, Morley," Mom says now. "Maybe the very best summer. Ever."

She parks in front of Jayden's house, then turns to smile at me. It's the way I'll draw her, I decide. Not sitting in the car, though. But definitely as she is right now, with the happy-mother smile.

Which makes me think, if I was going to draw the happy father smile, what would it look like?

......

"You know that rat thing you brought to school, Dumb-ass?" Julia is saying. Once again, I've made the mistake of not being with my friends when she corners me. She's standing too close, thumping me on the chest with one hand, clutching the collar of my coat with the other.

She's taller than me, and bigger, and almost a year

older. I can't get away.

I could spit on her, which is tempting.

"He's a cat," I say, "and you're stupid if you can't recognize what a cat looks like."

"Yeah, well it looked like something dead. But if it was a cat, it was black and disgusting. Don't you know black cats bring nothing but bad luck? Unless, that is, you're a witch, ha ha!" She thumps me extra hard on my right arm, which is still in a foam cast because it isn't healing properly.

Because Julia hit it.

I yelp in pain.

"And here's another thing you're too stupid to know, but I'll tell ya for free. Your mom's having another bastard, like you and that dumb sister of yours. Do I hafta to spell it out? She's knocked up! Preggers!" Julia grins, and I notice how thin her lips are. It's not really a grin. More like a curving snarl.

Then my brain kind of kicks in to say: What? My mom's pregnant? But...she can't be. Doesn't it take a father for that to happen?

"Yeah, go ahead and look all 'ooohh, I'm so little and stupid, I didn't know a thing...' " she says in that whiny fake baby voice that makes me want to smack her. "I guess that's not too surprising, with that creep who was hanging around. You know, Danny What's-his-name. The one that got arrested for stealing cars. And then that crazy guy who lived at your house. Everybody's talking about your trashy family. That's how I found out!"

I'm too shocked to reply. Mom is pregnant? Everybody knows?

Julia shoves me extra hard, banging my head against the wall behind me. "God, you're so pathetic you make me want to barf all over you!" she says, laughing but then, suddenly, there are some people playing with their dog nearby.

Julia just walks away.

But I'm shaking all over, and suddenly feeling sweaty and cold at the same time. And like I can't move. I feel myself slide down till I'm sitting on the ground.

The dog people come over and ask if I need help, but I say I'll be fine. I'm just tired. That's all.

So they take some more phone pictures of their dog and go away.

I stay there for what feels like a long time. Finally, I get up and start walking home. Wishing I had a phone, like they do. Like Sam and Jayden do. If I did, I could call mom or Eira to come get me.

Or if I had Spirit, he'd carry me home.

He wouldn't want me to explain what happened. Animals don't care about explanations, or reasons, or excuses.

He wouldn't ask a lot of questions about why my clothes are ripped and my bike is all bent up and I'm crying.

He'd know the way home. I'd climb on his back and he'd carry me there.

But I don't have Spirit.

And I don't have a phone. I'm in town, but there aren't any pay phones.

Julia knocked my bike over and stomped on it, so the wheel is bent. I expect I'll be in trouble for my bike getting wrecked. And being late getting home from going to the craft store for more bracelet-making supplies. When I promised I'd be back soon.

I walk really slowly, because I'm limping and hurting. And I have to push my bent-up bicycle, with the bags of the things I bought at the craft shop hanging off the handle bars.

Julia spread my bags all over and stomped on them, too. I haven't looked inside to see if what I bought is wrecked, like my bike. Because I've got more important things to worry about. Like what I need to ask my mother. What she's going to say, when I finally get there.

Part of me wants to be there now.

Part of me wants to never get home.

twenty-one

When I finally get to our house, there are two extra cars parked in our driveway.

I recognize one of them as Aunt Eira's truck. The other one is just the same as Mr. Maclean's. But why would the principal be visiting our house?

I push my bike into the garage and let myself in the side door.

"Morley?" my mother calls from the living room. "We're in here. Waiting to talk to you. Right now!"

Mr. Maclean is standing by the window, not looking at my mother.

She's sitting on the couch, looking angry.

Eira is in the side chair, drinking tea. Not saying anything.

But the real surprise is Julia. She has a cut on her face

and her jeans are ripped, too.

"Don't let her near me, Daddy!" she cries, sounding all girly, not anything like the real Julia.

I wonder what could have possibly happened to Julia to make her so...well, hurt looking.

She wasn't like that when I saw her, not that long ago.

I almost feel sorry for her.

Or maybe not really.

"Um...I just need to...go to the washroom," I say.

"Morley. SIT down!" my mother says in the voice that tells me I don't have any choice.

My head hurts and I really, really need to take a headache tablet and lie down, because I ache all over. There's going to be a lot of bruises. I just know it.

"Ok," my mother says. "Now, tell us where you've been and what you've been up to."

I tell them that I said I was going to the craft store for some jump rings and chain and some new glass beads and they had a coupon right now for the kind of needle-nose pliers I really want and I thought I'd get those..."

"Enough!" my mother says, "We don't need to know your shopping list. Then what did you do?"

"Well, I got on my bike to ride home, but..."

"But then you met up with Julia, here."

"Um...yes. Sort of. And..."

"And said some ugly things to her. About her mother..."

"No...that's what she said. I was..."

"You were what, Morley? And this better be the absolute truth from you. For once?"

What? What does that mean?

"I know you sneak around and keep secrets from me and bury your nose in all that drawing when anyone wants to talk to you..."

"Eefa. This isn't helping." Mr. Maclean says. "We just need to understand what happened. Today."

"Right," Mum says. "So tell us, why did you call poor Julia all those awful names? And say such horrible things about her mother dying? And then...I can't even put it into words. Then..."

"Then she says you attacked her." Mr. Maclean says. Why, Morley? Why would you do such a cruel thing? I really thought you were a better person than this!"

Behind him, Julia smirks at me. Her father, my mother and Eira are all looking at me, waiting for an answer. They don't even glance at Julia.

"But...it's not true. It didn't happen like that..." I say.

"Really," my mother says. "How did it happen that Julia, here, has a cut lip and scraped up knees and you were there? If it wasn't you who did this, who was it then?"

"I...um...I did meet up with Julia and..." She's looking really mean. I know if I tell the truth, she'll just beat me up worse next time.

"And I was just talking to her. And...um...I guess she fell or something and..."

"She fell? How?"

Right. How? Since we were standing on the sidewalk near the stores. Or where she shoved me, in the laneway between a couple of stores.

"OK. I think we need to leave Morley to think a bit about what the truth is, Eefa. Julia hasn't been raised to tell lies and, I'm sure, Morley hasn't either. But I need to get Julia home now. She's had a shock...

"But," he says, turning to face me, "I have to say how disappointed I am in this sort of behaviour from you, Morley. And I advise you to think very, very carefully.

"No, Eefa, don't bother getting up. We can see ourselves out. Come on, sweetheart..." and he puts a gentle hand on Julia's back and guides her towards the front door.

"So," my mother says when they're gone, "I can't believe you'd do such an awful thing. And have you forgotten, Morley, that Mr. Maclean is my boss? That he could easily find someone else to do my job? And that without my school job, we won't have a home to live in or anything to eat?"

I just sit there.

Without saying a word, Aunt Eira gets up and leaves the room.

"Well, what have you got to say for yourself?" Mom says. "And I'm warning you, if I catch you telling stories, I'll..."

"Are you pregnant, Mom?" the question pops out of my mouth before I can stop it. Or maybe I don't even want to try to stop it. "Are you having a baby?"

"We're not talking about that right now!" she shouts.

But that sounds like a yes to me.

But why wouldn't she tell us? Or does Daisy already know?

"And was Danny really a thief? Is that why he lost his job? Did he steal cars from the place where he worked? Julia said..."

Eira comes back with Daisy. She hands me a glass of water.

"What?" my mother says in her angry voice. "That's not what we're talking about. You need to do some serious thinking about your behaviour, young lady. "Go..."

"Fine," I yell back. "I'm going. Because, no matter what I say or what I do, you think it's always wrong. Everything Daisy does is right. Everything she does is good. You think everything about me is bad. You like her. You don't like me. That's just the way it is. And I just hate..."

"Stop NOW!" Aunt Eira roars. "Both of you. Before you say things that can't ever be un-said. Daisy, sit here with your mother. I have to talk to your sister."

I just hate being treated like this. Like I'm the bad kid. The liar. The bully. But also, the one who does all the work around here. Like I'm a servant, or something.

Not even a real person in this family.

Daisy is so surprised at Aunt Eira raising her voice that, for once, she does what someone tells her to do.

Mom just sits there, white-faced, saying nothing.

Eira steers me down the hall. She closes the door firmly behind us.

"OK," she says, sitting down on my bed and taking me into her arms. "It's OK to cry, darling. Cry all you need to…"

That's what I do.

A long time later, Daisy tries to come in to go to bed.

Aunt Eira says she's staying the night. She gives Daisy her pillow and her Frozen blanket. "You go sleep with your mother tonight, sweetie," she says, gently pushing Daisy out of our room. "Your big sister and I need to talk."

Slowly at first, and then with the words tumbling out, I tell Eira the whole story.

All of it.

I talk and talk and talk. It's like I can't stop, except to take another sip of water from the glass Eira gets for me.

Then I talk some more.

About Julia.

And the bruises.

And name calling.

And threats. To hurt me. Or kill me.

About my bicycle. Wrecked.

Danny. Why he doesn't write, doesn't phone us and doesn't come home.

My mother. Treating me like somebody she hired to do the baking and sell things at the market and look after the bed-and-breakfast guests. Or like a servant, to look after Daisy and vacuum the living room and load the dishwasher and all sorts of other jobs. Even though I've got bracelets to make. Drawings to finish. Homework to do and tests to study for, except in summer.

My father. Why doesn't he ever come to see us? Or even send a card or an email? From wherever he is.

Because I'm not allowed to know who he is.

But why not?

I don't remember when I finally stop talking. I think Aunt Eira must have taken off my shoes and thrown my blue quilt over me.

When I wake up during the night, she's asleep in Daisy's bed.

But I can't get back to sleep. I make myself a peanut butter banana sandwich and get a juice box and take them up to my room. What was my room. There isn't a guest in it tonight. It's all cool and shivery, with blueish light coming in from the moonlight.

I sit in the little alcove, pulling my quilt around me, at the desk. My desk. The one place in our house where you can sit and look out at the stars. They are especially bright and twinkly tonight over the ocean. To the East, there is one star that's the brightest. The most twinkly. I know it's the planet Saturn.

There's a full moon, with a creamy ring around it like a halo.

I eat my snack and wish I could just sail away, an explorer to the planets, finding far-away worlds of wonder.

I'd sail across that velvet sky, like the captain of a flying ship. Going where I want, guided by the halo moon and the bright stars.

Visiting stars in faraway galaxies. Just me. And Feather.

twenty-two

Mom barely talks to me for the next two days. I think she should apologize, but she doesn't.

Instead, she has an even longer list of things I'm guilty of. Like forgetting to gather up the recycling. Forgetting to put the garbage out. Or carry the laundry downstairs.

And letting Daisy try to cut her own hair with craft scissors.

And not unloading the dishwasher.

And upsetting my aunt with all those stories about Julia.

And, worst of all, she says, is not staying in my own bed and scaring her half to death because she thought I'd been kidnapped.

Which is stupid. How would someone kidnap me out of my bed and not wake up anyone else?

And why would anyone want to kidnap me?

But there is no use pointing this out. She says she's had about enough of my mouth. I'm grounded for two weeks. Which means no visits to Sam or Jayden. Or Aunt Eira.

No trips to the library or the beach.

No volunteering at the pet shelter.

No anything except still helping at the Saturday market and doing things at home, like looking after Daisy or cleaning or reading or making bracelets.

"Fine," I say. "Do what you want. I don't care!" And then I don't talk to her.

At all.

But I do think about calling the Kids Helpline. Because, isn't this bullying and abuse?

Telling me that what I think doesn't matter?

And that everything I say is a lie?

I think it is.

Eira says to cool off. "It's just your mum being a mother and worrying about you," she says. "Try to understand her. She has a lot on her plate right now." But why should I? She doesn't try to understand me. She doesn't try to understand anyone.

My aunt says I have to trust mum to do what's best for Daisy and me.

She says if I want to know about what Danny did, or didn't do, or about if my mother is having a baby, or even about my real father, I should just ask my mother.

As if that's any help at all. It's like me asking if I can have Feather. She never gives a real answer. Or any answer. All she says is, "Not now, Morley" or "Stop pestering me."

And isn't putting things off and refusing to answer the same as not telling the truth?

One day, when I'm eating my cereal and minding my own business, my mother says, "Well, you'll be glad to know that Mr. Maclean is dropping the complaint against you, Morley. He's decided this can be a learning experience for you. You're very lucky."

Aunt Eira has already told me that kids who are my age or younger can't get charged by the police, unless they do a really serious crime, like murder.

Mostly, when kids get in trouble, what happens is they're sent to get counselling. That means, figuring out what's wrong in their life. And they might have to do community service, which is like doing volunteer work. Picking up litter in the park. Covering up graffiti. Helping at the food bank. That sort of thing.

But that changes, Eira said, when kids are age 12, up to age 17. Then, they can be charged if they do a crime. Kids age 12 or older can be put on trial and can be sent to a special school for young offenders that's like jail for teenagers. Young offenders is what they call kids who are guilty of a crime that's proven.

I bite the side of my mouth to stop from saying what I really, really want to say to my mother. That all I did was try to defend myself. That Julia was the one who did the attacking. And isn't that a crime? And she's already 12.

Why wasn't my mother making a complaint about HER to the police? Why wasn't Julia being charged for attacking me? And other kids, because I know I'm not the only one she's hurt.

"A warning to you, Mr. Maclean called it," Mom says, continuing the lecture. "But we'll be going over to their house, so you can apologize. And you can take your bracelet money and buy Julia a gift, to show how sorry you are."

This makes me steaming mad. She is the problem, not me. But I still don't say anything. What would be the point? My mother doesn't believe anything I say.

She'd just shout at me and send me back to my room.

She's happy to believe anything that lying bully Julia has to say. Just thinking about it makes me want to punch something.

Instead, while she takes Daisy to the beach and tells me to behave myself, I make a quick phone call. "She's gone," I say, and hang up. Then I go out to the garage and pull out my poor bent-up bike. It looks like I feel. All beat up.

A few minutes later, Aunt Eira and Dom pull up. "Wow. This is worse than I thought," Eira says.

Dom just grabs my bike and lifts it into the back of the truck. "No problem, babe," he says. He's promised to fix it for me, if I make him a cool guy bracelet.

Sounds like a fair trade to me. Maybe better than fair. But then, Dom is a good guy. I'm glad he likes my aunt and she likes him.

I'm desperate to know how Feather is. I tried phoning the shelter to ask, but the person who answered is new. I don't know her. She wouldn't tell me anything.

If my bike was working, I'd go find out. Even if I had to sneak out. Because I really have to know.

"It's all right, Morley. We'll go find out," Eira says. "Right now. We'll be back before your mum and Daisy get here. We'll pick up something for dinner for all of us, how's that? What would you like, sweetheart?"

"Fish and chips," I say. "From Fry Daddy's. And a chocolate-mint milkshake. The giant size."

She laughs and gives me a hug.

I spend the afternoon alone, drawing. Painting. Making bracelets. Thinking.

Eira and Dom get back before mom, just like they promised. They say that Feather is doing fine. Just about healed. Apart from sneezing because he's got kennel cough.

Kennel cough is like a cold. Lots of pets at the shelter get it because they're stressed. Pretty much like people get colds, when they're run down.

Feather is four months old now. That's old enough to get adopted.

Just in time for my birthday, I think. Then I remember. I'll still be grounded during my birthday. I wonder what that means. If it means I won't be able to go to the shelter to adopt Feather.

Which means my mom or Eira would go get him. Because there's only one thing I've asked for for my birthday. That's Feather.

I already know I won't be having a birthday party, because my mom hasn't said anything about it. Which I guess is OK, because Jayden and Sam are both gone on their vacations. I couldn't have a party without them being here.

I try not to have these sad thoughts. Not when Eira and Dom are here, dishing up the food, which is vegan curry for Eira and pizza and fish and chips for everyone else, with mint ice cream if anyone is still hungry after all that.

We all sit down at the big table in the dining room. mom says that she and Daisy had a Big Talk about really exciting news, that she's getting a new little brother or little sister.

But what am I getting, I wonder? And why did she tell Daisy, but not me?

No one says anything about that. But it makes me feel like I don't really matter.

Like I'm invisible or something.

Dom sends me a kind look.

Under the table, Aunt Eira, who's sitting next to me, takes my hand and squeezes it. She understands.

Bastard. That's what Julia said. That word sticks in my mind. Aunt Eira says bastard is an old-fashioned word that used to mean someone who doesn't have a father. But in modern times, it just means a bad person. Or it's an insult word. Like swearing.

So, Eira says, it doesn't mean anything, except the person saying it lost their self control. They're angry, that's all. And don't know how to express themselves any better than using bad words.

So, am I a bastard? In the old way, not having a father. That looks like it's true, though I must have a father. Somewhere. Everyone does.

In the new way, a bad person. No, I'm not.

Is Daisy a bastard? She does have a father. Danny. And she isn't a bad person, just a really loud, annoying person.

Like a lot of little sisters.

Will the new baby be a bastard?

That is, bad person. I hope not. Probably noisy, though, like that baby who used to live upstairs.

Or a person without any father.

Or is Danny this new baby's father, too?

This feels like one of those questions that's just going to get me in more trouble if I ask it. But, luckily, I don't have to.

"And how does Danny feel about this?" Aunt Eira says.

Mom looks surprised. "Well, excited, I guess...happy, of course. You know how he dotes on Daisy. But you can ask him yourself. He's going to be here, next week."

Really? This is big news. Does it mean Danny's coming home? Did he find his new job here, in Seabright? Or near here?

I'm longing to ask.

Daisy is bouncing up and down in her seat, squealing, "Daddy's coming! Daddy's coming!"

Her daddy. The new baby's daddy. Not mine.

Mom and I are changing the bed in the biggest bedroom, what she's called the Garden Room because it's on the garden side of our house. It's faster when two people make up a bed. And a lot easier.

She's talking.

I'm still not talking to her.

"I know you feel bad about hurting Julia," she says. "But the sooner you own up to making a mistake, the sooner you can apologize and make amends. That's what has to happen, when you hurt someone."

Really, I think?

"So, this stubbornness and silence has to end, Morley, or so help me, I don't know what I'll do to get you to see sense, but I promise, you aren't going to like it!"

"She lied," I say. "I didn't. She did. She's the one who..."

"Morley. Enough. Just. Stop. We all know what you did. Mr. Maclean wouldn't have been over here, Julia wouldn't be hurt...but she is. And I'm losing patience with you!"

"Mr. Maclean...made a mistake. Julia did it herself!"

"That's it, Morley. That's absolutely it. You can stay in your room until …

I don't stick around to hear the rest.

In my room, I pull out my sketch pad. I'm still too angry to do any drawing. I lay on my bed and try to read.

Daisy comes in, but I ignore her.

She wants me to play Candyland with her.

"Go away," I tell her. "Just get lost!"

Finally, she does.

A long time later, I hear our car leave. That's when I come out and make myself a snack. And call my aunt.

Sam's mom has taken her to France, then Italy for their summer vacation. Jayden and his parents have taken their camper out to Ontario, where his brother Elyot is doing a hockey camp. Then they're going to drive to Vancouver. My two best friends are gone till August.

I don't have a phone, so I can't text them. But I can send emails from Eira's laptop. She keeps telling our mother that we need a computer at home. Mom says she knows about all that sexting and other trouble kids get up to when they have computers and phones and she's having none of it. She says I shouldn't even think of asking for a computer or a phone. It's too dangerous, she says.

And too expensive.

I've tried to tell her about the dangers of NOT having

our own computer or me not having a phone. That I can't do my homework. Or research new bracelet designs. Or buy my jewellery-making supplies like chain and wire and beads online, something Eira has already shown me how to do.

Or call when I need help, like a ride home.

Or to tell her where I am, if I'm staying after school for activities.

Or so she could call me, when she goes home early from work and wants me to do something, like take the bus home. Or start dinner.

As usual, she doesn't listen.

But I guess I'm lucky because Eira does. She says pack a few things, you're coming home with me for a couple of days. The weekend, at least.

This is a surprise. Maybe it's an early birthday gift?

"But Mom..." I say.

"I'll tell your mum where you are," she says. "Let's get you packed up, then what do you want to do today?"

I want to move in with Eira and Dom. I want them to be my parents.

That afternoon, we're sitting on Aunt Eira's tiny balcony. She's knitting, which is her new hobby. I'm making bracelets. And we're talking.

"You know your mum is pregnant."

"So that's why she's so angry and won't listen...?"

"No, not exactly. Just that...she has a lot on her mind.

And she has...well, she feels differently, because she's pregnant."

"She's got baby brain," I say. "And she's taking it out on me."

Eira laughs, but it's not her that's-so-funny laugh. It's her nervous laugh.

"Baby brain? Where did you hear that?"

"I don't remember. But isn't that what you get, when you're going to have a baby?"

I do remember, but Eira doesn't need to know. One of the things I really like about her is she always answers questions. Or at least tries to answer them.

"Your mum...has a lot of...well, pressure. She's worried about you. About all of you..."

"Yeah, she tells me all the time. She's worried about money. But she's making lots of money from her baking. There's all the people who buy it at the market. And now she's baking all the desserts for three restaurants. AND there's the bed-and-breakfast guests. We're full just about every night."

"True," Eira says. "Her two businesses are really successful. But that also adds a lot of stress. You know, Morley, because you're a business-woman yourself. It's hard work sometimes."

"Even when it's going really well?"

"Yes, even then. You worry that it won't always go that well, and of course, it won't. Just like life, there's good times and not-so-good times when you have a business."

I think about this. The silence stretches out, while Eira's knitting needles click and I finish another bracelet. It's one of the new man-style bracelets, made with leather. She nods her approval.

"But there's something different I want to talk about," she says. "It's about bullies and what you can do. To protect yourself."

"Like run away?"

"Yes, that is one way. Sometimes it works. But can you think of what else you could do?"

"Punch them and then run away?" What I'd like to do to Julia. Over and over.

"I hope you're joking," my aunt says. "Because, if you're serious, that just means you've sunk to their level. You're just as mean and cruel as they are. Hitting is never the answer. It just makes everything worse."

I'm not sure I agree. "Hitting might show them they better leave you alone. Or else."

"Or else what? They could hit you even harder and hurt you even worse. What then?"

"Then the adults take you to hospital and they go to jail."

"Well, maybe. In TV shows. Not in real life. And do you really want to go to hospital? You didn't much like it there last time, did you?"

This is true. "So what could you do?"

"Remember, a bully only knows one way to behave.

You have more choices in how you act and react to a situation."

"I don't know what you mean. You can run away, or you can let them hurt you? That doesn't sound like any sort of choice to me."

"You can run away. Or you can make it all into a joke. Or you can tell them they don't know what they're talking about. Or you can make sure to always have your friends nearby. Don't give them the opportunity to hurt you."

"To do that, I'd have to never go to school. Or never walk anywhere. Or ride my bike. Basically, never leave home."

"OK, let's say that's your choice. You never leave home. But do you really want to stay home all the time? Hiding there? Afraid to go out and do what you want to do? Like go to school, have your jewellery business, see your friends, have fun riding with Jayden or swimming in Sam's pool or going to the beach or the movies? Would you really give all that up?

"Is that what you want, Morley? To hide? That doesn't sound like you. I know you're a smart and brave and creative girl. So what else could you do?"

I don't get a chance to answer, because suddenly my mother is there, dragging Daisy behind her and roaring mad. "How dare you go behind my back and let Morley come over?" she's screeching. "You know she's grounded and I expressly said..."

"Calm down and sit down, Eefa," my aunt says in her

reasonable voice. "I think we all need to have a family talk. And we can't do it with you standing there yelling."

My mother stomps over, tries to grab me but misses and knocks my jewellery work-tray over. Everything tumbles to the floor.

I scramble around on the floor of the patio, trying to find all my beads.

My aunt leaps up, pulling my mother inside and pushing her towards the couch. "SIT. DOWN. NOW. And stop that screeching or you'll have me evicted!"

My mother is so surprised that she actually does it.

"Morley, you come in here too. Leave the beads. We'll pick them up later." I do that.

Daisy is playing with Pixel.

My mother looks like thunder. And also like she's catching her breath, getting ready for another temper explosion.

"OK," my aunt says. "Dom, can you get Eefa and Daisy some iced tea?" He looks happy to escape to the kitchen, leaving the living room to the girls and women.

"You had no right to let Morley come over and I don't know what got into her when she knows she's grounded..."

"Morley is my guest. As you are. And Daisy is. I invited her over..."

"She should have had the sense to say no. She should

have known better than to disobey my orders and..."

"And ask me for help?"

"Help doing what? Knitting?" My mother sips the drink Dom hands her, nodding her thanks.

Daisy has found a bright piece of string and is making the kitten run around in circles, trying to catch it.

I'm sitting there, wishing I could be somewhere else.

"Help telling you that she's being bullied."

"At school? That doesn't matter. All kids are bullied at school. A bit of name-calling, it's just part of growing up," my mother says. "Morley needs to get used to it. Grow a thicker skin. Toughen up. Not go around whining and telling tales..."

"If someone was beating you up regularly, would you say that's what you needed? They are assaulting you, and you just need to toughen up?"

"Now you're being ridiculous. No one is going to beat me up."

"No, they aren't," Eira says. "Because you're an adult. You'd know how to prevent it. Or how to put a stop to it."

"Yes, so...? What's your point?"

"That kids need to know how to prevent violence. They also need support to stop it when it happens. And, no, it's not normal behaviour. Not just name-calling. Dom, could you take Daisy down to get her an ice cream?"

Daisy beams. She's happy to go with Dom. And he

looks happy to be escaping all this family drama, too.

"OK," my aunt says when they've left. "I have just one more thing to say, and it's this. Morley, lift your top."

I don't want to do it.

"Morley, please. For me," my aunt says.

So I do.

"Now turn around."

I do that.

My mother gasps. "How on earth did you manage...?" she says.

"This isn't bullying," my aunt says. "This is assault. Now, Eefa, I can pick up the phone right now and call the police. Which I probably should have done sooner. Or...you can listen. And we can decide what's best to help Morley."

Aunt Eira turns to me, and now her voice is gentler. "OK, honey. I'm so sorry this is happening to you. It isn't anything you did to make it happen. It isn't your fault, not in any way.

"It isn't fair and it isn't right. But it has happened, it's happening now and you need adults to help you. This is an adult problem, not something kids can fix on their own. That's me and your mom. AND you. Working together..."

"But...Eira...we all saw..." my mother says.

She turns back to her sister, and says "Enough, Eefa. We know what you think. I think it's time you listen to your daughter."

Eira sits next to me on the couch. She takes my hands in hers. Her voice is gentle now and so low, I wonder if I'm the only one who hears her. "Tell your mother what you told me."

I don't know where to start.

"Begin with you were at the craft store. You bought some supplies. Then what happened?"

"Then...well, I got my bike, and..."

And I tell them what happened. While my aunt holds my hands and doesn't let go.

While my mother sits there, looking surprised.

Then shocked.

Then really, really angry.

But for once, she's not angry at me.

Instead, she asks some questions.

I answer, as best I can.

When I'm done, she doesn't say anything. And she doesn't try to hug me.

When she leaves, she takes Daisy and says that I might as well spend a few days at Eira's place. Since I already have my stuff here.

She says I'll need to still help her on market day, but otherwise she can manage. Eira says that she and I can do this Saturday's market and give my mother a day off.

My mother says, "thank you" to Eira. She isn't looking at me.

My aunt says, "We all need a bit of time to think. And cool off. And figure out what to do next. As a family."

I wonder what that will be. Will I have to go to the police and tell them what happened?

Will I have to change schools, to get away from Julia?

Or will she get sent to counselling, to make her stop the bullying?

Aunt Eira says she doesn't know. Partly, it's up to my mother. And partly, it's up to what I need.

I spend a week at my aunt Eira's. It's like a vacation, the best one of my life.

A working vacation, Eira calls it. She shows me how she does her blog and online store, and how it's also her job because it earns the money she needs to have her beautiful apartment and have a car and buy things.

She shows me more about using a computer. We look at videos of people making jewellery and I get lots of new ideas for things I want to make and sell.

Dom shows me how he does his work on a computer. He's a graphic artist. That means he does art and designs websites and some other cool things, all with just his laptop. He says I could learn how to do my drawing on a computer, too, if I want to. That way, I'd never need drawing paper or colour pencils or paint.

My mother says I can come home when I'm ready. And that there won't be any more being grounded. But I do still have to help out, she says. Because she can't do it all on her own. She needs me to help her.

She means with the guests upstairs and the baking business and looking after our family.

She says she's sorry for not believing me about Julia. She's sorry. She hopes I Can forgive her. I say I'll think about it.

I'd like to never be ready to go home. Just stay with Eira and Dom forever. But my aunt says that's not real life. And that my mother and I have to find ways to get along. Because, deep down, she knows we love each other.

So we have to see the best in each other.

And forgive.

We both have to try.

Even when it gets difficult.

Especially when it gets difficult.

Because that's what families do.

the end

Next In This Series:

Feather's Girl

As Morley Star's 11 birthday dawns she's convinced her wish to adopt the rescue cat she's fallen in love with will finally come true.

Surely getting Feather as her own is the big surprise her mother has promised?

But Morley is about to have a very different birthday and summer vacation than the one she's hoped for. There will be surprises and secrets revealed as she learns what it really takes to make your fondest wishes come true.

Read on to find chapter 1 of **Feather's Girl**:

one

On the day before my 11th birthday, Sam sends an email saying she hopes I finally get Feather. He's the kitten I want to adopt from the pet shelter. I'm pretty sure that getting him is going to be my surprise gift.

I've wanted to adopt Feather for so long, to finally get him is so exciting I feel like I'm going to burst with happiness, just thinking about it.

In just one more day.

It will be...

The first time I get to cuddle him at home. Our home, not at the shelter where he's been for three months.

The first time he sits on my lap, purring, while I'm drawing or making bracelets. Or maybe he'll want to sit on my desk and watch.

The first time he curls up beside me while I'm falling asleep.

I've pictured this in my mind and also in my sketch book so many times that to have it be true at last is...well, it's the best thing that's happened this year. Or maybe in my entire life!

Or it will be. In just one more day. Just one more. I'm counting the minutes!

Sam's letter says she's in Tuscany now, a place in Italy. It's where lots of movie stars have fancy homes. She's staying in one of them. It used to belong to a famous singer.

It's a palazzo. That's the name for a house that looks like a palace. She says she's having a great time. She sent my present and really hopes I like it.

Jayden, my other best friend, sends postcards with pictures of all the places they stop on their trip. He writes to say he's pretty tired of living with his parents in a little tin can trailer, but that it is interesting to drive across the country, especially when they were going through the Rocky Mountains. And he likes having so much time with his mom.

He says he mailed me a gift and to tell him all about my birthday. And how much he misses me and Sam and his horse, Spirit. But not school.

I've been away from home too, spending a week with my favourite aunt at her place. My Aunt Eira called it a time out for me and for my mother.

Things aren't much different at home. It's still hard to get along with my mother, and I don't think it's because she's going to have a new baby.

My little sister, Daisy, is still roaring around. My

mother is still cranky a lot, mostly with me. We still have the BnB guests to look after, and all the baking she does and the jewellery I make to sell at the market on Saturdays. We still don't know when Danny's going to visit, exactly. He's Daisy's father, but not mine.

Mom did decide to go to the police about me being bullied by Julia Maclean, a girl in our grade but she's a year older than me and my friends.

My mother took the pictures that Eira took of my front and my back and my arms, showing the bruises I got from Julia hitting me. I had to tell the whole story again, to the police.

But then a strange thing happened. Some dog-walking people who where there when Julia attacked me also went to the police. The man said when he looked more closely at the video they made that day with their phones, it looked like two kids were fighting in the background. When they looked really closely, it looked like one of the kids was that girl who did the videos about why kids need pets and pets need kids, and also how to get your pet that are on YouTube.

He meant me.

Then the police looked more closely at that video.

And saw that everything I been saying about Julia is true.

I wasn't the one who hit her and ripped her clothes and did the cut on her face, like she told everyone. She attacked me. Just like she has been doing since she moved here for grade 4.

It was embarrassing that strangers saw me getting beat up. And crying.

And to find out that the police showed that video to Mr. Maclean. That's Julia's dad. Also our school principal, or he was last year, at Seabright Primary.

My mother is surprised about the video.

She doesn't apologize to me about not believing me about the bullying. Not exactly.

But she does stop being mad at me all the time. And to tell the truth, I don't really want to talk about the bullying. Or not to her.

So I ask her about the new baby. She says she's happy about it.

She says she feels like it might be a boy, this time.

She says she knows it means extra work from me and she'll even expect Daisy to help out.

She says it is so exciting and wonderful for us to be getting a new baby brother. Or sister.

I don't ask her about Danny coming home any more. He's been gone for months and never comes to visit, though sometimes Daisy goes to see him. I figure Danny's not coming back to be with us. Even though I'm pretty sure he is the new baby's father.

I do ask my mother about my father. I've never met him. I don't even know his name or where he lives or anything about him. Usually, she just tells me never mind about him. So it's a surprise when she tells me that she loved him very much, once. When they were young. Maybe too much. And she thought he loved her. Just not enough.

He lived in Ireland, not here. When she knew him.

She has no idea where he is now.

She tells me his name is Malcolm. That's his first name. And she says maybe when I'm a bit older she'll maybe try to find him. Maybe we could search for him together. Some day. When I'm older.

She says maybe she should have told me this sooner. But she didn't think I was old enough to understand.

She says she worries that I'm still not mature enough to understand. That's why she won't tell me his last name, she says. Because it could just stir up trouble.

But she knows where he lives. Or used to live.

Doesn't that mean he knows where we live?

But then why doesn't he come to visit? Is he a bad man, maybe even in jail so he can't come to Seabright to see me?

Or just someone who doesn't like kids? And doesn't even want to be a dad?

What if he's a good guy and he's tried to find us, but he can't?

Mom just shrugs when I ask. I think maybe she knows the answers, or some of them. But she doesn't like to talk about things, or at least not things I think are important. She'd rather talk about making cookies and what we need to do next for the guests that stay at our house and what chores I have to do next. You know, ordinary stuff.

I don't ask her about Feather. I think getting him must be my big birthday surprise. I don't want to spoil it.

I wake up on the day of my birthday really, really excited. Today's the day, finally, when I KNOW I'll bring Feather home. I'm so sure that's what I'm getting, because the wish bracelet for getting him broke, didn't it? That's the magic about wish bracelets.

Even though it was Julia who broke it on purpose, I think my wish bracelet should still work. Because that's what wish bracelets are meant to do. They break and then the wish you made the very first time you put them on comes true.

I've made hundreds of them and sold them at the market. That's what I always tell people who buy them.

Everything is ready for Feather to come home. I have his litter box set up and food dishes and food and some toys.

I've got the pet carrier, to bring him home.

And I've read all about having a cat and what they need and how to care for them. Because of the Get A Pet Project, I know a LOT about cats. And because of being a volunteer at the pet shelter, I know a lot about being a responsible pet owner.

I hurry through breakfast and try to make Daisy hurry, too. I know the pet shelter opens at 10 a.m. We're ready long before that.

But then, my mom just starts baking. And says we can go get whatever it is I want for my birthday dinner.

There's no party. I already knew that. How could I have a party without my two best friends being there? Most of the kids I know are away for vacation. Aunt Eira and her boyfriend, Dom, have gone up north to his parents' cottage for two weeks.

My other aunt, Sorcha, and her kids have also gone away, to see their grandparents in Winnipeg. There's nobody to celebrate with except my mother and Daisy.

The three of us go out for lunch. I get to pick where. I choose the Peony Garden. It's got Chinese food. I really like the chicken fried rice and you get fortune cookies.

As I'm chewing my honey chicken, I wonder what Sam and Jayden are doing right now. Probably not eating lunch, because it's a different time where they are. I know, because I looked it up. Time for breakfast where Jayden is now, out in Vancouver. It's already night in Paris, where Sam is. I really wish they were here.

My fortune cookie says, "You will soon receive a gift of great riches." I haven't been thinking about being rich. I want a gift of great furriness.

Daisy's says, "Sweetness and joy will light up the days of your life." I guess that's already true for her. Mostly. She's already as happy as her name, when she's getting her own way.

Mom doesn't say what her fortune says. She just reads it, frowns and says, "They're just silly," and stuffs it in the pocket of her shorts.

After we eat, she pulls out a bag of gifts. I wonder if we're going to the shelter to get Feather right after lunch. Or if he'll already be at home when we get there, because she says the big gift from her and Daisy is at home, in our room.

My gift from Sam is a wire jewellery-making kit with lots more bracelet designs in it, plus a gift certificate to the craft store. Jayden sent me a book of funny facts about pets and a poster of kittens and cats.

Mom says I can choose what colour frame I want for my poster. Danny sends a card with money in it and so does my grandfather. Mom says that can go straight to my bank savings account.

Eira and Dom also got me a card. Inside, there's a certificate for 12 art lessons with Maudie Lewis, a local artist whose work really blows me away. I'm super excited to meet her and get to paint with her.

Daisy gives me a card with lots of fairies playing with dancing kittens. It gives me an idea for a bedtime story for her. But maybe, this time, I should write it down and draw it, like a graphic novel. Or, better yet, let her draw it.

Now that it's summer, one of my jobs is thinking up fun stuff for her to do so mom gets lots of baking time and some rest time. Daisy drawing a book of fairy pictures could keep them both happy for a while, I think.

When we leave the restaurant, we drive to the craft store, where I pick out some more jewellery-making supplies and a frame for the poster Jayden gave me. Then I think we must be going to the pet shelter. But instead, mom turns towards home.

"Look in your room to find your gift," she says when we get there. "I know you're going to love it!"

I run down the hall. "Feather?" I call. "Feather?" I look all over, but don't see him. And I don't hear him, either, in my head.

Is he hiding? I can't tell.

My mother comes into our room behind me. "Isn't it pretty? I really hope it fits," she says.

It fits? Then I see it, on my bed. It's a new bathing suit with green and purple splodges and huge pink and red flowers. And there's a matching stretchy beach skirt. And a pink sun hat. And a new pair of sunglasses. And a bright pink tee shirt, with a skinny white cat on it. The cat is wearing ink sunglasses.

"I know how disappointed you were that you couldn't swim at your friend's party. But that's the last cast you're going to have on your arm, so soon you can swim again. I know you've missed it. I thought you'd love a new suit."

It's just about the ugliest bathing suit I've ever seen.

"So, are you going to try it on?" Mom says. "Isn't it so cute?"

No, it's not. It's hideous. Like the most ugly wallpaper you've ever seen. Times a thousand. But you're never supposed to say that, about a gift.

I don't know what to say. It isn't anything like what

I'd pick out, if I was going to get a bathing suit, which I'm not going to put on. Not until the bruises are gone. Plus, putting on a stretchy tight thing like a bathing suit is still really hard, with one good arm and one kind-of weak arm in a cast.

I might be able to get it on. But, after swimming, when your swimsuit is wet and plastered to your body, it's even harder to get off than it was to get on. I'm not going to let my mother or anyone else help do that.

"But...it's not Feather." I say. "You said wait-and-see about getting him and I did wait. And wait. For a really long time. So I thought..."

"Feather? What are you talking about?"

"Feather, the kitten..."

"At the shelter? No, Morley. I told you, we aren't getting any pets. So please just stop whining about it. Believe me, I have my reasons for no pets. Very good reasons..."

"What are they?" I say, shoving the ugly bathing suit aside so I can sit on my bed. I wish she'd just take it back to the store. "Because I explained for every single reason you had to say no, there was a way to not have that problem. It was all in my pet project presentation. Everything, even how I can pay for Feather, so I thought you ca..."

"I'm sorry, Morley," she says, interrupting me. "Listen to me. Now isn't the right time to get a cat. We've just had a lovely lunch out together and you have some beautiful gifts. Why don't you have a look at them?

You need to remember to be grateful for what you've got. And you have some Thank You letters to write too, don't you?"

Thank you letters are another rule at our house. You have to write them the same day you get a gift. Just saying, "Hey, thanks," in an email isn't enough, Mom says.

That would be if I could send an email. There's no computer rule in our house, and I'm not allowed to use her phone. Also, I can't have my own phone.

I'm so disappointed, I want to cry. Or maybe yell at someone. I'm too upset to make jewellery, or draw something, or read, or do anything.

"Yeah," I said. "Maybe. Later. I'm, uh, going for a walk..."

"Fine. Be back by 4, because we're going to the beach. I promised Daisy..."

I grab my bike that Dom fixed almost like it was after Julia stomped on it and head for the pet shelter.

There, I check on Feather. He's still in his cage, curled up, falling asleep.

Feather, I'm sorry. I'm so sorry, I tell him in my mind.

Girl. Gone, he says. Then he's sleeping.

I race through all the tasks they ask me to do, watching the clock. I get those jobs for the other pets done in record time, so I can have a long, long cuddle with Feather. I wash my hands and lift him out of his cage. I sink my face into his soft fur. His head smells like carnations and cinnamon.

Girl, he says.

Morley, I remind him. I'm Morley.

Want to go home, he says. Take me home.

He starts to purr. He has a really soft purr, so soft you have to be cuddling him to even hear it.

He looks up at me and puts one soft white paw on my cheek.

I whisper to him about what it will be like, when he comes home with me.

When he is mine.

And I am his.

I promise him that it will be soon. I say it out loud. Because I need to hear it. I need to believe.

Most of all, I need to hope.

Continued in **Feather's Girl**

About the Author

Jacquelyn Johnson writes books for curious and creative kids ages 8 to 12.

She used to work as a newspaper and magazine writer and editor. Her articles and photographs have appeared in newspapers and magazines in Canada, United States and Britain.

Jacquelyn is also a former teacher, college and university lecturer. She has taught English as a Second Language to children and teenagers in South Korea and journalism to university students in South Dakota and Ontario.

When not writing, she enjoys watching her garden grow while doing as little actual garden work as possible, re-decorating her home with shabby chic finds (that means fixed up used stuff, a hobby she shares with Morley's mother, Eefa) and music.

She grew up studying piano and later played the trumpet, though regrets that she has never learned to play as well as Sam Park. Or make jewellery as well as Morley. Or ride horses, like Jayden can.

She makes her home and garden with her family near the ocean in a town very much like Seabright. Just down the street from a house that's very much like Morley's. With a little cat who's very much like Feather.

CPSIA information can be obtained
at www.ICGtesting.com
Printed in the USA
LVHW050202211220
674730LV00003B/227